ELIE WIESEL was born in Hungary in 1928. He was deported with his family to Auschwitz when he was still a boy, and then to Buchenwald, where his parents and a younger sister died. NIGHT, his first book, is a memoir of these experiences. After the war he moved to Paris, where he adopted the French language and assumed French nationality. His work as a journalist took him to Israel and finally to the United States, where he now makes his home in New York City. His books include *DAWN, THE ACCIDENT, THE TOWN BEYOND THE WALL, THE GATES OF THE FOREST,* and his most recent, the internationally acclaimed *A BEGGAR IN JERUSALEM* (winner of the French Prix Mediçi for 1969).

THE TOWN
BEYOND THE WALL

Elie Wiesel

Translated from the French
by Stephen Becker

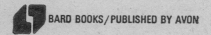

BARD BOOKS/PUBLISHED BY AVON

AVON BOOKS
A division of
The Hearst Corporation
959 Eighth Avenue
New York, New York 10019

First Printing (Avon Library), July, 1969
Fourth Printing (Bard Edition)

AVON TRADEMARK REG. U.S. PAT. OFF. AND
FOREIGN COUNTRIES, REGISTERED TRADEMARK—
MARCA REGISTRADA, HECHO EN CHICAGO, U.S.A.

Printed in the U.S.A.

I HAVE A PLAN—TO GO MAD
Dostoevski

First Prayer

OUTSIDE, TWILIGHT SWOOPED DOWN ON THE CITY LIKE a vandal's hand: suddenly, without warning. On the red and gray roofs of the squat houses, on the living wall of ants surrounding the cemetery, on the nervous, watchful dogs. No light anywhere. Every window blind. The streets almost empty. In the square near the Municipal Theater only Old Martha, the official town drunk, exuberates. She has the whole city to herself, and her performance unfolds in a kind of demoniac ecstasy. She dances, flaps her voluminous skirt, displays her naked, scabrous belly, gestures obscenely, shrieks insults, flings her curses to the four winds. Joyfully she prances before the universe as if before an audience, her mirror.

"What did you say?"

Michael opened his eyes. The voice was the voice of a man who was not of the city. It brought him no memories, no richness.

"Nothing," he said. "I didn't say anything."

He returned to his pictures. The butcher removes his blood-blotched apron: there will be no more customers today. In the grocery across from the church a peasant girl crosses herself and murmurs a prayer. In the main square the horse harnessed to the baker's green cart whinnies nervously. He too is tense, alert. Above, the fist squeezes tighter, tighter. The city seems to want to shrink. The houses contract; the trees narrow. Another danger suddenly becomes apparent: the mountains that surround the city. It might be the end of the world.

"What did you say?"

"Nothing," Michael answered. "I said nothing."

"I heard you mutter something."

"I said it was the end of the world."

"It'll be the end of you, if you don't make up your mind to spit it up."

Behind him the officer's voice was calm, fresh, barren of any hint of impatience or even interest.

"You're a bloody fool," the officer went on. "You think you can take it. You think you're tough. Others have thought so before you. A day, two days, three . . . in the end, they talk. And you will too. You want to wait? All right with me; we'll wait. I have plenty of time. You want to play games? We'll play games. But I warn you: the game's rigged. You lose. You've already lost. In this room you get talkative in spite of yourself. Soon—maybe in an hour, maybe in three days—you'll start screaming and shouting. You'll be begging for the chance to make a long speech, to get rid of it all. Every minute makes the load heavier. You'll feel it in your legs. Here it's the legs that turn talkative."

The storm broke suddenly. Bolts of lightning zigzagged across the sky. The wind screamed like countless raging beasts. The officer stopped talking, and Michael went back to his city. He didn't care for slow rain, but storms fascinated him. He loved to watch nature let herself go. At sea he always wished he could be alone on the bridge, alone to contemplate the unleashed waves. On land a storm brought him out into the streets or fields. Even now he saw himself walking down toward the main square, listening to the groans of trees whipped by the wind. Old Martha is there. She dances, she sings, she shouts, she pirouettes as if she wanted to be one of the elements, part of the chaos. Suddenly she seems to be aware of this very fact and stops abruptly, dumbstruck. For the space of a second the beast holds its breath. The storm stills upon her lips. Then, as if at the old drunkard's command, the thunder revives and the night again spews its fire and flame.

"Who are you?" Martha shouts.

Michael remains silent. She frightens him. Ugly, her body ravaged and faded, she is so old that in the city they take her for her own great-grandmother.

"What's your name, little boy?"

Michael is entranced by the desiccated face. He has never seen her this way. Children liked to run along behind her and throw stones at her, but as soon as she turned they fled, an exhilarating terror prickling their heels. She chased them hotly, shouting, "You'll burn in hell. Your children will die young. Your tongues will fall in the mud. And your eyes with them . . ."

"Don't you want to tell me?"

"No."

"Why not? Are you afraid of me?"

"Yes."

"And what is it about me that scares you?"

There is only a brief space between them. Michael promises himself: if she takes one step toward me I'll run. "They say things about you."

"What things?"

He lowers his gaze, uneasy. "That you're a witch. That you're Satan's wife. Lilith, wife of the king of devils."

"And you believe it?"

"No, not all of it. Lilith is beautiful and young and seductive. I know. It says so in books."

The drunken woman does not seem to appreciate the highly moral compliment. She sparkles with fury, shakes a fist at the little boy; her voice grows sharper, scratchier: "You little fool! I *am* beautiful and young and seductive. Come, make love with me, see how my body is beautiful, how my blood is young. Come! We'll make love right here, in the street, in the gutter. You'll be the center of the universe, the heart of the storm! Well? What do you say?"

Michael's breath comes harder. Legs wide apart, the old woman glares at him, mocking. "Well?"

"I don't understand," he answers.

"What don't you understand?"

"Love."

"Nobody understands it. You define it by what it isn't. Love is neither this nor that, but something else. Always something else."

"And make love? What does that mean?"

"To make love, little boy, means to pretend to love. Even that's a lot."

The old woman takes a step toward him. Fear fastens upon him. He is about to flee. She notices. Her eyes become glowing coals: "Leaving me, are you? You don't want to stay here with me? Then listen to what I have to tell you, listen well. Yes, I sleep with Satan, yes, I'm his wife and his lover. Yes, I carry his child in my belly. But I'm not like other women. It takes me more than nine months: *my* child is the whole world—you, your friends. And I keep my child with me, in me, in my belly, a hundred years, a thousand! *You're* in my belly, all of you. You stink of my blood, you're tangled in my guts. And you think you're pure? You call yourselves clean? You disgust me! So much that you make me laugh!"

With that she spits in the mud, and Michael, only eight, nine, ten years old, spins away and runs. He is soaked to the bone. Luckily he lives not far off. Four blocks. In the house on the corner of Kigyo Street and Kamar Street. His parents are doubtless waiting for him, worried; he should have been home from the *cheder* a long time before. Michael wonders how he'll explain the delay to them. He would like to think it over, and prepare an answer, but Martha is pounding along behind him, fury on her lips: "I'll get you! You won't get away! I'll be despair on your tongue and drought in your heart! At night I'll live in your miseries and by day I'll freeze your sun! You'll be damned, turned away everywhere, I promise you!"

Quickly, luckily, Michael remembers a prayer that gives men power over the messengers of Ashmodai, King of the Shadows; he repeats it again and again, *Shadai yishmereni vehatzileni mikol ra.* The Almighty will protect me from all evil. Suddenly he can no longer hear the drunken woman's steps behind him. And anyway here is the house. Panting, he kisses the mezuzah and opens the door. Instead of his father, a voice welcomes him: "Haven't you had enough of praying?" It's not his father's voice. Michael is astounded. Who is it, then? And why does that man speak to him in Hungarian and not in Yiddish?

"Not finished praying yet?"

The dream burst into a thousand pieces. The cell, the wall, the officer's monotone voice. How many hours have passed? These jumps from one world to another had killed all sense of time. No more landmarks. It could as easily have been one hour as seven. Not eight, anyway. That he deduced from the fact that the first officer was still there. He knew that after eight hours another officer would relieve him.

So this is The Prayer, the famous prayer, Michael thought. The torture, named by an erudite torturer, consisted of breaking the prisoner's resistance by keeping him on his feet until he passed out. The torture bore the name of prayer because the Jews pray standing. The prisoner is stood face to a wall; he stands there day and night. Forbidden to move, to lean. The prisoner may close his eyes and even sleep —if he can manage it without touching the wall. Forbidden to cross his legs. Every eight hours they escort him to the bathroom, and when he is brought back he finds a new officer on duty. Most prisoners break within twenty-four hours.

The colonel to whom Michael had been marched immediately after his arrest by the Security Forces had said to him point-blank and almost with kindness, "Don't be a fool. We know who you are. We also know that you're not a spy. Your rashness proves it. Our counterespionage agrees. So why be stupid about it?" The colonel had extraordinary eyes: green, cold. A sensual mouth, delicate lips. A thin mustache accented the sharp lines of his face. His black hair was graying at the temples. "Answer two questions and I'll consider the interrogation finished. Why did you come back? And how?"

Michael turned him down: "All I can tell you is that you're right to think I'm not a spy; I'm not. No one sent me here to do anything. My reasons for coming back are strictly personal, and there's nothing military or political about them."

Michael knew that the conversation would not end there; that they would torture him. He also knew that he would not be able to hold out for too long. He had no illusions about himself. He confessed to cowardice and weakness. Able to confront moral torment with his head high, he was afraid of physical torture. A body is not so easily controlled. Still, he declined the bargain. He thought of Pedro and kept silent. He re-

membered his friend's face and his lips remained
shut.

"In that case," said the colonel with the cold eyes,
"I am obliged to force you to say a few prayers."

"They'll do me good," Michael said.

"You think so?"

"Yes. It's been some time since I last prayed."

The colonel remained impassive. In a glacial voice
he resumed: "These prayers break the toughest men
—or perhaps I should say the toughest legs. You
finish them defeated and humiliated. You run the risk
of losing your mind, faith, honor, and pride. I advise
you to talk. You're young, innocent; don't sit in on a
game you've lost in advance."

But Michael sees Pedro. His sad, full laugh.

"You like to talk about God?"

"You know I do."

"Then go on. Go on, Pedro. Talk to me about God."

*"God, little brother, is the weakness of strong men
and the strength of weak men."*

*"What about men? Do you like to talk about men
too?"*

"You know I do."

"Then talk to me about men."

"Man is God's strength. Also His weakness."

Michael sees his friend's eyes. Deep-set eyes, where
joy and despair wage a silent, implacable, eternal battle. And he says to himself, no, I will not betray. You
hear, Michael? You will not betray. Three days is a
long time, but you'll hold out. After that it won't matter. Pedro will be out of danger. He'll come to the
meeting place; I won't be there. He'll understand and
he'll go. Just don't let him try to find me or wait for
me. No nonsense, Pedro! Three days is a long time!

"What have you decided?" asked the colonel, his

eyes so green and cold. Seeing that Michael did not stir, he went on: "As you wish. We have plenty of time."

He pressed a button. A policeman escorted the prisoner to the basement where several "temples" had been arranged.

"Not through praying yet?"

It was still the first officer's guttural voice. So it hadn't been eight hours. Maybe two, maybe seven. Outside, the storm had subsided; a weary rain drizzled down. Michael felt fine. Altogether lucid, in perfect possession of his thoughts, his memories, his inner resources. He commanded them, and exacted obedience. His powers of concentration had never afforded him so much pleasure. He went so far as to draw a small satisfaction from his arrest. Without it he would never have known this mastery of the most obscure recesses of his consciousness, of the deepest withdrawn impulses of his body. It was enough to say, "I will not think of my legs," and he did not think of them. "And now I'm going to visit the Mellah in Casablanca," and there it was, an enclave of misery surging up out of the past with its silent old men (blind, you would have said, so ponderous, so real, was their silence), its badly dressed, underfed little girls, their poor cheerfulness breaking your heart; its one-room dwellings where families of twelve, thirteen, fourteen barely existed. "I want to see Sarah, and there she was, dragging her smile like a heavy load, spitting her scorn in the face of centuries past and centuries to come. "Master, come to me!" and there was Kalman, at his service: the old man, beard streaked yellow, who walked always with bowed head (for we must not waste our eyes). Michael can speak to him, propose questions and demand answers. "Master, I want finally to know God. I want to drag him from his hiding place." The master replies gently, without anger, in a very soft, very clear voice: "You are presumptuous, my son. You want to know God: do you yet know yourself?" Michael retorts: "Not yet, Master, not yet. But it won't be long. I can feel it. Another day, two, three, and I'll know myself. And don't be offended, Master; I'll know the unknown, too: God. In prison, under torture, man becomes powerful, omnipotent. He becomes God. That's the secret: God is imprisoned!" At that the master casts a sweet, sad glance at him, illuminated by a mysterious orange glow, and says, "You may be right. In our time the disciples know more—and better—than their teachers. Yes. God is imprisoned. Man must free him. That is the best-guarded secret since the Creation." Michael wants to learn more about it: "Is that why so many good men go to prison?" "That's one of the reasons." Michael is still unsatisfied: "And thieves? Murderers? Traitors? Why do they go to prison? Do even *they* know God is locked up in there?" The master wags his yellow beard: "They know it. They go in because of that. To do away with him." Michael sees that his master is tired. He takes his leave with respect, kissing the master's hand.

They say of the celebrated Rabbi Schmulke of Nicholsburg that once a year, on the eve of Passover, he locked himself in his room and allowed no one near his door. He required to be alone, listening, eyes shut, to the voices of his disciples, calling to him from the four corners of the earth.

Michael can do as well. He need only lower his eyelids to perceive the sounds of the past. Michael goes even further: senses in himself a force the Zadik of Nicholsburg never possessed (he was never in prison): by closing his eyes Michael contrives not only to hear voices, but also to see faces, movements, men at grips with their destiny, with their very lives.

Pedro had asked me, "What do you call that city with the barbarous name?"

"Szerencseváros," I told him. "Which means the city of luck. Don't make fun of it, Pedro. I was born there."

"Is that what the luck was?" Pedro asked, laughing.

"Don't make fun," I answered, hurt. "Don't ever make fun of a city that has had enough luck to live through so many foreign occupations and changes of government. Every power in Europe, large and small has been after it. Sometimes it seems to me that Szerencseváros was the real stake in both world wars. First it was part of Austria, then it was ceded to Hungary, which gave it to Rumania and took it back twenty years later. Then Germany claimed the honor of incorporating it into the Third Reich—which permitted the U.S.S.R. to take it away from her a short time later. So the forty thousand people of Szerencseváros never knew exactly to what country they owed their faith and allegiance. You see, Pedro: you can't make fun of such a fabulous city, desired by every government in Europe."

But Pedro isn't the man to change moods so quickly: "And now who occupies it? Maybe Monaco?" And he let himself go in a laugh like the roll of a hundred drums, punctuating it with his favorite exclamation: "It's fantastic, fantastic!"

I was sad. I was always sad when I recalled Szerencseváros, which means the city of luck. But Pedro was my friend. He felt no need, no duty, to join me in my sadness. If he felt like laughing, he laughed.

He stopped abruptly, and lowered his voice: "Have you ever gone back?"

"No."

"Why not?"

"I don't like graveyards. And the city of luck is just that: a great cemetery. And lying in it are faces and

legends, holidays and hopes, the brooding dark eyes of sanctity, prayers sent up to tug a tear from God himself."

Pedro became thoughtful: *"That must be quite a cemetery. A fantastic cemetery."* He was no longer laughing.

Up against a range of high, impassable mountains and flanked by two rivers as wide as oceans, Szerencseváros was a small city, happy and poor. Even the rich were poor there, and even the poor were happy. Happiness in Szerencseváros came down to its natural expression: enough bread and wine for the Sabbath meal. So the poor toiled six days by the sweat of their brows, that they might have bread and wine for the seventh.

Like a mantle of purple silk the Sabbath came to drape the city at sundown on Friday. The city's face changed visibly. Merchants closed their shops, coachmen went home because there were no passengers, the pious proceeded to the ritual baths to purify their bodies. The Sabbath is compared to a queen: it is proper to have body and soul clean, to merit her visit. The Sabbath: the essence of Judaism. The divine revelation in Time.

Through half-open doors and windows the same song of welcome spread through the deserted streets: "Peace upon you, O angels of peace; peace upon you as you come and peace upon you as you go."

Friday night in Szerencseváros no one goes hungry. Even the most impoverished family has something on the table covered with a snow-white cloth: bread, wine, and lighted candles, one for each living soul in the family. Whoever is alone, whoever is a stranger, is invited by the people of the city to come and break bread with them.

Friday night even Mad Moishe, the fat man who

cries when he sings and laughs when he is silent, even
he will taste the holy joy of the Sabbath, and its
peace: he is much in demand. In choosing one invitation over another, Moishe behaves as though he were
conferring a favor.

A family without its poor guest at table feels uneasy, guilty. As soon as prayers end at the synagogue,
the faithful rush upon the beggars, upon the strangers. In Szerencseváros the poor consider themselves
important; they permit the rich to be happy without
shame. When Friday night comes, Yankel the Hunch-
back, who dies of famine all week long, becomes
Someone; people notice him, immerse him in kindness, battle for his favor. They are the angels of peace
of the Sabbath: the poor, the dispossessed.

Mad Moishe came often to dine with Michael's
family; Michael's father was his intimate friend. The
young boy had never quite understood what really
linked those two men, of whom one believed only in
the power of reason while the other resisted all clarity. Michael saw them chatting often: Moishe spoke
and Michael's father listened, now amused, now serious.

One day Michael asked his father, "What do you
find in him, to spend so much time talking with him?"

"Moishe—I speak of the real Moishe, the one who
hides behind the madman—is a great man. He is far-
seeing. He sees worlds that remain inaccessible to us.
His madness is only a wall, erected to protect us—*us:*
to see what Moishe's bloodshot eyes see would be
dangerous."

After that Michael too tried to talk to the fat man,
who needed two chairs to sit down. But Moishe
would not accept the little boy as someone to talk to.
"If you want to hear me sing, all right," he said.
"Talk, no."

"But I have questions I want to ask you," Michael begged.

"Keep them to yourself," Moishe answered.

That went on for months. The madman sang or was silent. He did not speak. And Michael, fascinated, burned with curiosity. He became convinced that Moishe bore a secret within him, an unknown message, perhaps an answer to the eternal questions. So Michael never stopped trying.

And then, one evening, the much desired conversation took place. It was in winter. Michael was alone in the house (his mother and father were in the shop) when Moishe loomed in the doorway, looking undone. Later Michael learned what had happened. The children of the town—who bore him a cruel love —had made him drink urine, telling him it was wine.

"Give me some wine," Moishe said.

Michael opened the cabinet and took out a bottle. He set it before his guest. "I'll bring you a glass," he said.

"No need." Moishe threw his head back and drank the bottle empty. "It is written," he said in grieving tones, "that wine brings joy to the heart, and felicity. It's false! My heart is empty of joy! Empty of wine!"

Without a word Michael opened a second bottle. This time too Moishe picked it up abruptly and drained it into his throat. "I am not joyful!" he cried furiously, flinging the bottle against the wall. "The wine brings no joy to my heart. What is written in the books is false! Like the wine. The wine is false too! Like the heart. The heart is false too!" Tears gushed suddenly, and were lost in his bushy beard. "You," he said, "you, you don't know anything. You're too little. Too young. But I know. I'm a madman and in this base world only madmen know. They know that everything is false. Wine is false, the heart is false, tears are false. And maybe the madmen are false too."

Lost in thought, his eyes shut, he was silent for a long moment. Michael thought he had fallen asleep. But the tears were still running. Red tears, wine-colored. The boy took a chair and sat down, careful not to wake the sleeper.

"You can make noise," Moishe remarked. "I'm not asleep."

Michael blushed as though he had done something discreditable. He would have liked to shrink to nothing, to disappear beneath the table. Eyes still shut, Moishe asked him, "You're afraid of me?"

"No."

"But I'm Moishe the Madman. Aren't you afraid of crazy men?"

"No," Michael said.

"That's good," Moishe said. "You should never be afraid of other people, even if they're crazy beyond the pale. The one man you have to be afraid of is yourself. But immediately the grave question arises: who says that the others aren't you? Who says Moishe the Madman isn't you?"

Michael never budged. He clung to the chair as if to keep from toppling off.

"The others!" Moishe cried, bringing a fist down on the table. "The others! By what right are they not crazy? These days honest men can do only one thing: go mad! Spit on logic, intelligence, sacrosanct reason! That's what you have to do, that's the way to stay human, to keep your wholeness! But look at them: they're cowards, all of them! They never say, 'I'm crazy and proud of it!' But they jump at a chance to yell, 'He's crazy! Moishe's crazy! Keep away from him!' As if every one of them wasn't at some time in his life another man, called Moishe, Moishe the Madman!"

Raging, the fat man breath heavily. His powerful voice was full of fury. But his tears witnessed his sadness. Suddenly he half-opened his eyes to the boy, who found infinite kindness in them. Moishe leaned forward and tried to smile: "You're still not afraid of me?"

"No," Michael said, quivering.

"The truth?"

"I'm afraid, Moishe. But not of you. I'm afraid but I don't know of what."

"I like you. You don't lie. You're nice. You're intelligent. Just like your father." He tugged at his beard, as though he were angry, and shouted, "I'm going to sing for you."

He put a hand over his eyes, the better to drop into the chasms of memory. Tears ran between his fingers. "I'll sing for you. What would you like to hear? A prayer for Yom Kippur? For Shavuot? No. An older song. A love song. First let me tell you the history of this song. Rabbi Yitchzav Eizik, the famous shepherd of Kalev, was walking in the woods one afternoon when his ear was struck by the words and melody of an infinitely sad, infinitely beautiful song. He followed the voice and discovered the singer. It was a young Hungarian guarding his flock. 'Sell me your song,' the rabbi said to him. 'I offer you twenty crowns. Will you accept?' The young man stared at the rabbi, uncomprehending. 'Well, will you take it? Twenty crowns? Thirty? Forty?' The young Hungarian stretched forth a hand, and the rabbi dropped fifty crowns into it. At that instant an astonishing thing took place: the song fled the Hungarian and was received by the rabbi. The one had forgotten it, while the other had learned it, and that in less than a second. Later the rabbi explained to his disciples that this love song, composed by David the King, had wandered for many centuries, waiting to be 'liberated.' . . ."

And leaping to his feet with surprising grace, Moishe paced the room, chanting the *Szól a kakas már*, a feverish, nostalgic song in which the lover implores his distant mistress to wait, to wait even until God consents to unite their separated hearts. Moishe had a hoarse voice, full of warmth and chagrin; it seemed to surge up out of the shadows, amazed by its own power.

When he had sung himself exhausted Moishe sat down, wiped his wet beard on the back of his sleeve, and asked for a little more wine. Michael set a third bottle before him. Moishe looked up at the boy: "It seems to me you have questions to ask. What are they?"

"Some other time," Michael said. "You're tired."

Without knowing why, Michael felt nervous. Even knowing that the chance might never come again, he hesitated. He examined his fingernails, head bowed.

"Go ahead," Moishe encouraged him. "Don't put things off until later: they change too fast."

"I can't," the boy said. "You make me shy."

"Look at me," the madman said. "I order you to look at me."

Hesitant, Michael raised his head slightly.

"More than that."

And when the boy did not obey, he went on: "You must never be afraid to look a man in the face. Even a madman. Ask your father. He'll tell you."

That's his secret, Michael thought. He's not crazy. But in that case the others are. And me? What am I? Moishe or the others?

"Look at me, I tell you!"

Michael wished to obey, but his head seemed heavy, heavy, as if it had changed weight and shape, as if it were the head of a stranger. Finally Moishe had to take the boy's chin in his hand and raise his head for him. "Don't close your eyes! Don't raise your brows!"

Michael saw such deep shadow, such a concentration of night in Moishe's pupils that he was dizzied.

"Don't look away!" the madman cried angrily, froth flecking his lips.

For a long moment Moishe and Michael stared at each other without a word. It was Moishe who broke the silence: "Now you'll never forget me." His voice had become calm again, and was drifting toward silence.

"I have no more questions," Michael said.

"Fantastic!" Pedro exclaimed. "I would have been happy to know him."

"Yes, Pedro," I said. "You should have known him. You'd have loved him."

"What's become of him?"

"Ashes."

Pedro was still. Then: "You think he was afraid of death?"

"Moishe wasn't afraid of anything." After a silence: "Not even madness."

Pedro started to laugh again. I was sad, but he was laughing. Maybe that was how he showed sadness.

"You never asked him any more questions?"

"Never."

"You understood everything?"

"No. But I had no more questions to ask him."

Pedro slapped me hard on the back: "I have."

"Go ahead."

"Moishe wept as he sang: why? He laughed when he was silent: why?"

To explain that I had to paraphrase something from the illustrious author of the Tanya:

"When he sang, Moishe was heartbroken; that's why he wept. But when he was silent he mused about the ancient truth that nothing in the world is as whole as a broken heart: that's why he laughed."

Pedro stared hard at me and said, "You were lucky to meet him. Too bad he's dead."

"Too bad, yes. But he wasn't afraid to die. I'm sure he went to his death singing; I'm sure he took his song into the other world. And his madness too. God loves madmen. They're the only ones he allows near him."

My friend's eyes softened; they were seeing Moishe the Madman, a fat man who always sat on two chairs.

"You know what I like about him?" he asked.

Pedro spoke of Moishe as if he had known him, as if the madman were still alive, there, with us; Pedro spoke the same way of all my dead friends: he gave them immortality.

"What do you like about him? His voice? His songs? His movements?"

"No." Pedro shook his head. "I like his laugh."

And he winked.

Three days, Michael told himself. I must hold out for three days. My legs have to hold up for three days. Seventy-two hours. Less three, four, five, six, or seven hours. Say five. Sixty-seven left. Don't be afraid of anything, friend. I'll hold out. But afterward, keep going. Run. Don't start looking for me, tracking me down. If I'm not at the meeting place by the cemetery, you'll understand. You'll understand that I won't be able to follow you again; my legs will be too heavy, like dead wood.

Michael became aware of his exhaustion. His head ached. He couldn't dissolve a thick paste in his mouth. His throat felt dry as leather. But most of all he felt his legs, from the knees down. A strange humming reached his ears. Mosquitoes. They were swarming around his legs by the thousands. Soon he would feel a tiny sting, then another, then another, then nothing: the mosquitoes would have devoured his flesh from his knees down.

And I was so amazed at the customs of the Parsees, Michael thought, because of the strange way they disposed of their dead. They confided them to the birds of the sky, and not to the earth. The Parsee priests, after the customary prayers, stretch the body of the deceased on the summit of a tower called the tower of silence, on a specially constructed platform. Then they clap three times. On that signal hundreds of vultures wing up from the surrounding trees and blot out the sky. They rush upon the corpse. Two hours later nothing is left on earth of what was once a man. Horrible! That had been his reaction when he learned the customs of Zoroaster's disciples.

Michael heard the mosquitoes preparing their attack—they will begin at the legs and rise to my head. He smiled: I am not a Parsee, but I will have the death of a Parsee. Man's liberty does not, apparently, extend as far as his death. He chooses his life, but his death is imposed upon him from without.

At least I'll die on my feet. Most creatures huddle before their death. At its approach, they shrivel; they wait for it like vanquished men, their shoulders touching the earth. Not I! I'll welcome it on my feet. Even Moses, the only man who ever saw God, didn't have that luck. Michael remembered a legend of the Midrash on the death of the Jewish Liberator. God bade him, "Lie down." Moses, who had seen the Promised Land from the peak of Mount Nevo, lay down as God had asked. "Stretch out your legs." Moses stretched out his legs. "You can no longer feel them." Moses could no longer feel them. "Stretch out your arms." Moses stretched out his arms. "You can no longer feel them." Moses could no longer feel them. "Close your eyes." Moses closed his eyes. "You no longer see." Moses no longer saw. Then God ordered his heart to stop. So the slow death of the first of the prophets was consummated.

Mine too will be slow, bit by bit. First my legs will die, then my haunches, my arms, my heart. But I'll die on my feet. And Pedro will be saved. That's always the way it is: when one man dies on his feet, another is saved. Sometimes it's a friend, sometimes an unknown, born tomorrow.

Three days. Three times twenty-four. Seventy-two hours. No: sixty-seven. Michael is unafraid. Time doesn't terrify him. He can escape from it. It is enough to close one's eyes: the mosquitoes will leave them, at least, whole. Eyes are stronger than mosquitoes, stronger than death.

To conquer time, and plunge back into the past, attentive to its voices, its cries, it is enough to close one's eyes. A man hears really well only when his eyes are shut.

When Michael saw old man Varady in his garden, his heart raced. He had never seen a man so old, or so pale.

Varady lived in the house next door. The two gardens were separated by a wooden fence. Varady's land was out-of-bounds for the boy. On that point his parents had been absolute: "Forget about Varady! Forget the very existence of a man named Varady! Forget that anybody lives in the house next door! Erase his name from your memory!"

"But why? Why?" Michael was astounded, of course.

"Don't ask so many questions," his mother said, more anti-Varady than his father. "When you're grown up you'll know."

"What could he have done, Varady? What does it mean, this *no*, this mystery?"

His parents denied him enlightenment: Varady didn't exist, and no one explains the nonexistent. Naturally, that only sharpened the boy's curiosity. He spent hours at the window or in the street, spying. But the neighbor never came out. Michael had even begun to wonder if the mysterious old man really existed, when he saw him by chance through a gap in the fence. Then the boy was already twelve years old.

It was a scorching summer day. But Varady seemed to be trembling with cold. He huddled in an armchair beneath an apple tree; only his head, startlingly white, was outside the blankets. He wasn't asleep. His gaze, filtering between barely open eyelids, were fixed upon infinity. Michael was taken with pity for that old man with the eyes of a dying dog, whose body no longer soaked up the sun's rays. Like a burglar, his heart pounding, he pried the nails out of a slat, contrived an opening, and slipped through to the other side of the fence. Once in the forbidden garden he stopped, frozen in timidity, not knowing if he dared go on. But it was too late to retreat: the old man had seen him.

"Come closer," he ordered in a scratchy voice.

Michael bit his lips and obeyed. He stepped forward. Now it was easier to make out the face before him. The skin was so transparent that he could see every bone.

"Who are you?" asked the old man, impassive.

Michael spoke his name and added, "I'm your neighbor."

"What do you want here?"

Embarrassed, the boy stammered.

"I didn't understand," the old man said. "Repeat. Repeat what you just said."

Michael, who was already regretting his disobedience, made a great effort: "I wanted to see you."

"Why?"

The boy was silent.

"Why did you want to see me? Come, come, answer!"

"I don't know, sir."

"You force entry into my garden, you stare at me, you observe me, perhaps you judge me—and you don't know why?"

"No, sir. I don't know why."

The old man thought it over briefly and then leaned forward: "Tell me, little boy; what do they say about me outside? What are the people saying about me?"

"They say you don't exist."

The old man laughed. The muscles of his face rippled, and Michael though he heard a crackle. "So that's what they say," the old man murmured, as if to himself.

"Yes," Michael repeated. "They say you don't exist."

"And what else?"

"That's all. They say there's nothing to say about a man who doesn't exist." Michael felt his voice fall back to normal. Of all the emotions Varady had roused in him, only curiosity remained.

"Do your parents know you're here?"

"No."

"Will you tell them?"

"I don't know. Maybe."

"You'll tell them you've seen me? And that I exist?"

"Maybe."

The old man's voice dropped: "Don't do it. They'll punish you." He paused and then repeated, "Don't do it. Keep the secret for yourself. What would life be worth without our little secrets?" His lips were seized with a violent trembling; his face flushed purple.

"Do you want some water?" Michael asked.

Varady gestured, yes. On the low metal table beside the old man Michael found a bottle of water and a box of medicine.

"Do you want a pill too?"

Varady nodded again. Michael poured water into a glass, extracted a pill from a phial, and handed both to the old man.

"Thank you, little boy," Varady said after a few minutes. "Were you afraid? Afraid I'd die right here in front of you?"

"Yes," the boy admitted. "I was scared. I've never seen a man die."

"I've seen them die." Varady grimaced. "It's not pretty. That's why the dead feel guilty. Not to God, but to the living. Guilty for offering a melancholy and ugly spectacle. There's nothing sadder, nothing uglier, than a corpse. Or more of a nuisance. I'd like to die like the prophet Elijah: he flew to heaven with all his earthly burden. I have no desire to leave my body behind." The skin of his face was quivering: he was telling himself a funny story. Finally his eyes returned to the boy. "I'm old," he said. "Isn't that right? I'm old."

"Yes, sir."

"How old would you think?" the old man asked in a grotesque, teasing tone.

"I have no idea, sir."

"I'm over a hundred."

Michael couldn't hide his surprise: "Really? Over a hundred?"

"That's a long time, isn't it?"

Michael let himself stare at old Varady's face; the old man was like a ghost, or a fossil. His eyes were interesting: Varady never quite closed them all the way. It was as though he were afraid he would never be able to open them again.

"What are you thinking of, little boy?"

"I was wondering if I'd ever be that old."

Varady left the remark hanging in the air. Timidly, tenderly, a breath of wind tossed the leaves of the apple tree. Some day, Michael thought, I'll understand the language of trees and the wind too: it must be like the language of old men.

"What do you do with your days?" Varady asked.

"I study. The Bible, the Talmud, and Latin too."

"Latin?"

"Yes. Because of my parents. They're always arguing about me. Mother wants me to be a rabbi. Father would rather have me study for a doctorate in philosophy. They're funny, my parents. My mother lives body and soul for Hasidism: she devotes her actions and thoughts to God. My father adores reason: he devotes all his time to skepticism about the eternal verities. To make peace between them I promised to study religion *and* philosophy."

Varady was listening, his eyes half shut, and Michael wondered again if he was awake.

"That's dangerous," the old man murmured.

Michael, still standing, leaned forward slightly to hear more clearly.

"It's dangerous," the old man said again. "To swear fidelity to both light and shadow is to cheat. Of the roads that lead to truth there is never more than one. For each man there is only one. In that sense the atheist and the mystic are alike: they both proceed directly to the goal without turning aside. At the goal, of course, they meet. But if their paths cross on the way, they run the risk of canceling each other out. Do you understand, my boy? You can't be inside and outside at the same time. Man is too weak, his imagination too poor, to enter the garden and yet remain beyond the wall. I know something about that. . . ."

Michael was struck dumb by the unexpected rush of words. The name of Elisha ben Avuya plucked at his memory. The illustrious Elisha ben Avuya was the master and teacher of the great Rabbi Meir, of whom the Talmud says that on entering the "orchard," which is to say the tabernacle of esoteric knowledge, he lost his faith. Could it be that this desiccated body, emaciated by a century of anguish, was inhabited by the wandering immortal soul of that great wise man, who had risked not only his reason, but also his faith, in his passion to learn what can be discovered only within oneself?

"Yes, I know something about that," the old man went on after a pause. "It's dangerous, I tell you."

The boy burned with curiosity. He guessed, suddenly, that there was a direct link between the words he had just heard and the wall erected by his parents to protect him from the old man.

The day was ending. The light, clear as crystal, was fading into blue. On the heights of the mountains the sun tipped pines with flame; as if to salute that miracle of beauty, churchbells began to strike six.

It was then that Michael sensed a strange presence behind him. A girl, blonde, gentle, very poised, was watching him silently and with some amusement. She was fourteen or fifteen at most, but there was something mature in her manner.

"You're the first visitor Monsieur Varady's had in a good long time," she said.

"I hope I haven't bothered him too much," he answered, blushing.

"No, no," the old man interrupted. "You haven't bothered me at all."

"My name is Milika," the girl said. She shook hands with the boy. "I take care of Monsieur Varady." She smiled. "They also call me the orphan. That's because I never knew my parents. Monsieur Varady knew them."

"That's Michael," the old man said in his bird's voice. "Be nice to him, Milika. He hasn't given up trying to understand either, poor boy."

"At his age?" She was astonished.

Michael, uneasy, seemed to be present at a conver-

sation where people talked about him without noticing that he was there. He hardly dared breathe.

"Will you come back?" Milika asked warmly.

"May I?"

"Of course you may," the old man said. "You know
the way. Third slat from the left. Let's just hope you
find me still . . . among the living."

During the weeks of summer that followed Michael
multiplied his clandestine visits to his strange neighbor. He came to admit a real affection for that forbid-
ding death's-head, for those eyes beaming narrowly
out at the world. Varady asked him questions, told
him stories, spoke of books and writers with remote,
obscure names. Now and again Milika glided near
and joined the conversation, and at those moments
Michael felt the warmth of her gaze burn against his
lips.

One day Michael lost patience and burst out,
"Monsieur Varady, why do they hate you in this city?
What have you done to them? What crime have you
committed?"

The old man made odd sounds; Michael could not
tell whether they were whimpers or growls, whether
the old man was weeping or vastly amused.

"They hate me, you say? You say they hate me?"

"Yes, sir. Not with words: they hate you in silence,
as if they wanted to make the hate last, so it would
pass from generation to generation. When your name
comes up their faces shut tight. You can almost hear
their teeth grinding. I want to know why! What have
they got against you? What have you done to them?"

Sitting on a small taboret across from the old man,
Michael observed him carefully. Varady, expressionless, seemed suddenly to have gone a great distance
away. Even his breath was imperceptible. A few moments passed in motionless silence; then the old man
opened his mouth, and Michael trembled.

"I am immortal," Varady said.

The boy understood then that a man could be cold even in a red-hot oven. His blood froze.

"Don't be afraid," Varady added. "I'm not insane. I still have all my faculties. And no one in the city will deny that. They don't accuse me of insanity, but simply of immortality. That's the sap that nourishes their hate. Men don't reject death, but they do immortality. Even God, they only desire Him insofar as He's mortal: they kill Him often to prove that to themselves. They only love a God capable of suffering, of bleeding, of dying. They understand only what is limited, fleeting, subject to the laws of time. Everything must be in their image, made to their measure. But I love men only when they shatter their mold, when they assault the immutable barriers of the past, present, and future; when they possess the strength and courage to impose their will on the universe, on death. I love men to be strong; but they prefer to be feeble, crawling. That's why they hate me: I jolted them. I shook the ramparts that defended their cowardice."

Hardly daring to move, Michael awaited the rest. But Varady broke into a cough. He shook so violently that Milika came running to take him back to the house.

A few days later Michael found the orphan alone in the garden—and depressed. Varady was confined to his bed. The boy wanted to leave, but the girl held him back. They sat on the grass beneath the apple tree. Alone for the first time with that beautiful creature, her face glowing with tenderness, serenity, kindness, Michael felt awkward.

"What a strange character, the old man!" Milika said.

"He is," Michael agreed.

"He likes you very much."

Michael blushed. "Me too. I like him."

She looked at him with so much warmth and affection that Michael averted his eyes.

"Talk to me about him," he said. "Do you know him well?"

"Very well. I've been caring for him for two years. He sent for me, to a village where I was living with my grandparents; they were very poor, and quite happy to have one less mouth to feed. Since then I've taken care of him. And you know, taking care of an old man is almost like being his mother; it's like having a baby, with all the age behind, instead of in front." As she spoke she took Michael's hand in her own. He dared not pull away.

"Do you think he's crazy?"

"Oh, no!" Milika exclaimed. "He's the sanest man I know."

A new sensation was invading Michael. Blood rushed violently to his head. His heart seemed swollen. When she stroked his hand she raised goose flesh. He was awakening suddenly to pleasure—to a pleasure which was, at the beginning, strangely like pain. "Tell me, Milika. You're his mother, and you should know: is he immortal?"

"A bit, like everybody," she answered, laughing.

"Don't make fun of me. I was asking seriously. He said it himself."

Milika was silent, dreamy; a subtle melancholy washed her features. "It's a joke," she said finally. "An exasperating joke. All his jokes are exasperating." She stroked the boy's hand, then his hair, the back of his neck, his chest; Michael was so nervous that it required a great effort to keep from fleeing altogether. "Varady adores jokes," Milika went on. "He'd sell his soul for a good joke, a good, exasperating joke. Maybe that's the secret of his long life: he can turn his life into a joke. Just by the fact that he's alive, he annoys people. It's not what he does that makes them hate him; it's his life, the breath of his life."

Later, from his father, Michael learned the surprising facts of the old man's past: descended from a great rabbinical family, he had taken the name Varady to spare his people shame. And yet until he was eighteen he had honored that name. His teachers had conferred upon him the prestigious title of *Illui,* which means both genius and sage. He knew the whole Talmud by heart. And the commentaries. And the commentaries on the commentaries. He was not yet fifteen when he earned the *Smicha,* the title of Rabbi. He was the glory of the district, and they had predicted that he would be a new Gaon of Vilna. The most illustrious rabbis sought him as son-in-law. The change came in his eighteenth year. He set about the study of the *Zohar* and the other books of the cabala. For three years he never left his room. He imposed perfect solitude upon himself. He ate alone, prayed alone, refused to receive anyone, including his father. They left his meals on a little wooden table near the door; next day they found the dishes, often untouched, in the same place. During that time of isolation no one had set eyes on him. Now and then one or another of his friends caught a glimpse of his blurred silhouette through a window. He was like a shred of night dreading the arrival of day. Then one evening he opened the door and walked down to the synagogue, to the ground floor, where dozens of students were chanting their study of the Talmud by the light of candles. When they saw him a sudden silence fell over the room, so complete, so crushing, that the walls seemed to crack beneath it. "Tell the others that I intend to speak this Saturday." Then he turned in his tracks and went back to his room. A few minutes later, while the rumor of his return spread through the city like fire, his father came to knock at the door.

He paused on the sill, pale and trembling. Father and
son took stock of each other for a long moment, as if
measuring the abyss that three years had hollowed
out between them. It was the son who broke silence:
"Father," he said, and his voice cracked in his afflic-
tion, "I ask you not to come to temple this Saturday."
The father blanched beneath his beard; his eyes
flashed briefly: "Are you sure you have not overesti-
mated your strength?" he murmured. The son opened
his mouth, but did not speak. Then the father stepped
back, and hastened away. That Saturday the whole
city, save only the father, was at the synagogue. No
one had ever seen such a multitude, so vast an audience. The great men of the Yeshiva were there in full
panoply, and their disciples with curly side locks; the
rich were there, and the workers, the shoemakers, the
coachmen and the tailors; they all came with their
wives and children. In the place reserved for women,
on the floor just above, the air was suffocating. It was
in the morning, between the prayer of *Shaharit* and
the prayer of *Musaph*, just after the reading from the
Torah. The young man stepped up to the pulpit with
perfect calm and examined his audience, which hung
upon his least gesture, upon the motion of his lips.
The three years of isolation had rendered him more
mature, more handsome, more tormented, more re-
fined also. Following the ancient custom, he took the
Sidrah of the week as a point of departure and then
plunged into the Talmud. Upon one verse of the
Bible he erected a temple, with all its turrets, its
stained-glass windows, its walls, its silences. It was a
masterpiece of rhetoric. Women wept without understanding a word of it. But his voice was beautiful,
deep. It carried far. The first to show signs of uneasiness were the great men of the Yeshiva and a few of
the elders. They raised their heads, as if the better to
grasp and define what charmed their ears. And sud-

denly they understood that the orator would stop at nothing, not even blasphemy. His quotations from the Talmud, from the book of Ezekiel, from the *Zohar*, from the *Sefer Hayetzira* which is the book of the creation of the world itself, one after another tended in the same direction: blasphemy. The thing seemed to them so incredible, that is, impossible, that they permitted the young man to continue. His face inflamed, his gaze upon infinity, he was at any rate approaching the end. There could be no doubt: he was lost. He emphasized the strength of man, who could bring the Messiah to obedience. He claimed that liberation from Time would be accomplished at the signal of man, and not of his Creator; the irony and beauty of it was that "each of you, the men and women who hear me, has God in his power, for each of you is capable of achieving a thing of which God is incapable! It is enough to forge the Will, to hammer it, to temper it, and thus to free it! Man is not what he does, but what he wishes! He will conquer heaven, earth, sickness, and death if he will only raze the walls that imprison the Will! And I who speak to you announce here solemnly my decision to deny death, to repel it, to ridicule it! He who stands before you will never die!"

Michael's father went on: the temple was totally stupefied. A bolt of lightning could have had no greater effect. The silence was prolonged, and lay heavily on the frozen audience. Then the great men of the Yeshiva, followed by the elderly Talmudists, sprang to their feet. Their strength surging back, they brandished their fists and shouted, Blasphemy! Blasphemy! They tried to mob the young man, but he escaped without harm in the confusion. He did not go home. That evening, secretly, he fled the city, leaving not a trace. He undertook long journeys, studied at Paris and at Heidelberg, spent some years in an ashram in India, performed a pilgrimage to Tibet, where he lived in a monastery among the lamas. When he returned, thirty or forty years later, he bore the name Varady. A certain number of those who had heard his oration were still alive. The rabbi, an uncle of his, sent an emissary to ask if he had repented. "Tell the rabbi," Varady cried, "that I remain a Jew. At no time did I deny my religion or my people. But I still hold, and more than ever, that man is more important than God; that it is in no wise a sin to aspire to immortality, even at the cost of deposing God. Tell the rabbi that I shall survive him, and his son too." Naturally he was not reintegrated into the community. Some considered him a renegade, others a heretic. No one crossed his doorsill. The only man who had come to visit him, just once, was Gabriel, the convert to Christianity; Varady chased him away. He lived alone, on the fringe of humanity, but he lived: that was the essential. He was ignored; they pretended he did not exist; but in the depths of its soul the whole city listened, measuring his heartbeat. Varady rejoiced in all this.

Generations passed, the rabbi joined his ancestors, and his son died in turn, but Varady was still there. Each time a citizen died Varady seemed to invest him with a meaning, a message for those who attended the funeral: "Very disrespectfully, Varady wants you to know that he still lives, that he will survive all of you, just as he has survived me!"

Summer was drawing to an end.

The High Holidays were near. The month of Elul, the month of penitence. Every morning, to the harsh sound of the shophar, the faithful at the synagogue rendered an account of their sins, beat their breasts, and implored forgiveness.

Michael knew that his visits to Varady would end

with the arrival of winter. He would not have time. His studies would fill his hours.

One afternoon he found Milika under the apple tree. She was reading. He sprawled beside her. The orphan closed her book.

"Varady is sick," she said. "He has to stay in bed." She added, "It's better that way. I wanted to be alone with you."

The boy did not answer. He trembled within. He felt sick, feverish, lacerated by an unfamiliar anguish. Alone with a woman: wasn't that a sin? Milika took his hand and brought it to her mouth; her breath was a warm, gentle breeze. Michael closed his eyes, not to see the earth gape beneath them. He was falling, a dizzying fall, down, down, toward hell. He had just been given the first kiss of his life.

Suddenly his heart almost stopped: strange yet familiar sounds had become audible, like groans of pleasure or whimperings of pain. An image leapt to his mind: Varady! He couldn't be far. Through his narrow, slitted eyes he was watching, savoring the scene he had set. . . . "Be nice to him, Milika. . . ."

With a rush of strength he pushed the girl away, freed himself from her embrace, jumped to his feet, and raced out of the garden, gasping, not looking back, as if Satan or his wife, the beautiful Lilith, were pursuing him.

"It was a joke," I said. "An innocent joke. I was twelve."

My friend slapped me fondly on the back. "And if I know you, you never went back. Right?"

"Right, Pedro. I never set foot again in the forbidden garden."

Pedro hauled out his pipe and filled it attentively. He concentrated. Whenever he very carefully followed the mechanical motion of his fingers, stuffing the pipe slowly, delicately, it meant that he was distracted, prisoner of a thought. "Don't stop," *he said.* "Go on. Keep talking."

"What do you want me to talk about?"

"Her. Milika. You said she was beautiful?"

"Very beautiful. A welcoming kind of beauty, full of promise and offering. In one hand she held a storm, in the other, peace; she offered them at the same time."

"Could you have made love to her?"

"I don't know."

"Think. Yes or no?"

"I think so. But then the joke would have been perfect."

"Are you sure? Sure it was a joke? Sure you didn't run purely and simply because you were afraid? Afraid of committing a mortal sin? Afraid of being happy and sharing that happiness with a woman, at the very moment when you were sinning against God? Afraid of finding Good in Evil?"

I knew I was turning pale. "Shut up, Pedro," *I begged him.*

He had finished stuffing his pipe. He put it between his teeth and lit it. Then he looked up and stared at me. He seemed to be saying, Speak; I won't judge you.

"I remember a story Varady told me one afternoon. He was talking about his travels, his women, his discoveries, his victories, his defeats. 'Do you know what I regret most in the world?' he asked me. 'Not having made love to a girl who invited me to. I was fifteen or sixteen them. My parents had taken me along on a vacation to the mountains. We stayed a month. I spent most of my time in long, lonely walks. I got up early to be there when dawn broke, to watch God at work. I liked the sure, inevitable way of the sun: giving form to the pines, to the valleys, to the rivers, to

living things. I compared it to human thought: that
too envelops all, and brings forth from the darkness
things, events, and ideas. One morning I was the victim of an unexpected apparition. I was busy watching
the sky turn purple on the horizon, when I had the
feeling that I was being watched. A young woman,
her hair and body still draped in night, stood motionless watching me. She was not far from me: a few
steps at the most. I hadn't seen her arrive. She
seemed to have fallen from heaven or sprung up out
of the earth. Neither of us made the slightest movement. For several moments we stood petrified, staring
at each other like two creatures brought together after
a long separation. And then she broke the spell. Without taking her eyes off me, she began to undress.
Naked, she waited. Erect, motionless, she waited for
me. And I couldn't tear my eyes away from her body.
I was still religious, very pious. I was preparing myself for asceticism, and within me I knew that to look
upon a naked woman was a sin; but I didn't stir, I
didn't close my eyes, I recited no prayer for God's
help. There was thunder in my blood, my innards
churned; I went on staring. Then she stretched forth
an arm and signaled me to come to her. At that moment the entire universe was a woman's body. Her
body gave the sun its light, its heat, its strength.
Seeing me rooted to the spot, she stretched both arms
toward me. I was so forcefully drawn to her that I bit
my lips to keep from crying aloud. At just that instant
the sun rose behind her. The girl, arms outstretched,
seemed wrapped in a veil of blood. That bloody tint
tore me out of my stupor. I turned and went away,
trying hard not to run. Well—I cannot erase that girl
from my damned memory. She is still there, always
there, before my eyes, her out-stretched arms laden
with the dawn. The other women I have forgotten, or
I can forget them when I want to. That one, no. She

never moves. She is still waiting for me to come nearer, to take her, to unite myself to her, within her. I should have done it, that morning on the mountain. Perhaps a great many things would have happened differently. . . .'"

Pedro, the pipe in his right hand, looked tense. The two blue veins in his temples were swollen. He waited for me to go on. When he saw that I'd finished he broke into uproarious laughter. His face was still tense, but he laughed, slapping his knee with his left hand. "Ah, what a joke! What a marvelous joke! I like your Varady. I like the way he talks. He deserves immortality!"

His laugh died as suddenly as it had burst out. He set the smoking pipe at his feet, stood up, and brought his face close to mine, his eyes close to mine: "Tell me this," he said in a tight, throbbing voice. "Is it for him that you want to go back to your city? To see if he's still alive? If he's really immortal?"

Standing before him I felt unnaturally heavy. My legs were breaking at the knees. I wanted to fall down. But I managed to stay on my feet, rigid; I met his eyes without flinching.

"No, Pedro," I said to my friend. "It's not that."

"You mean you never dug for the end of his story? You don't care what happened to him, to his immortality?"

"I don't mean anything like that," I said to my friend. "The end of the story, the material, tangible end, I know. Varady is dead. Yes, dead. He died a few days before we left the city. Being a Jew, despite his age, he was to be deported. It didn't happen, because he was no longer alive. But—one thing. Before he killed himself—yes, it was suicide—he made Milika swear to keep his death a secret. He wanted to make his legend last. It was Milika who told me about it later, in Paris."

Pedro breathed heavily; he said nothing. Then he leaned forward and looked closely at me and in a very soft voice asked, "Why, then? If not for him, why this desire to go back in time? Why, Michael? Tell me. I promise to understand."

I was trembling from head to foot. Thousands of mosquitoes were jabbing small needles into my legs. My head was heavy on my shoulders, like a separate burden not my own.

In face of my silence Pedro stooped, picked up his pipe, and stuck it back in his mouth. He had to light it again.

The officer was talking:

". . . so swollen that we had to cut his pants open with scissors. As I told you. Pig-headed, he was. Stubborn. Kidding himself that he could tire us out, wear us down—us. One day, two, three. Maybe he was telling himself that his stubbornness would make us admire him and win him a pardon. Big mistake. All we felt was disgust and scorn. You have no idea how ugly, how grotesque a man becomes after a couple of days. I told you: his legs were so swollen that we had to cut open his pants. With scissors. They were like columns, his legs. To get him to the bathroom every eight hours we had to carry him by the shoulders and legs. That strike you as pretty, a man you can't tell from a corpse?"

The officer yawned indifferently. Michael was cold. From which he deduced that the night was well along, that the guard would soon be relieved, and that they would take him to the bathroom. He would be able to revive his numbed limbs. And to warm himself. He turned up the collar of his jacket and for the first time looked like a prisoner.

He tried to move his legs. The right, then the left. They felt heavy, but they responded to a serious effort. The mosquitoes had not yet devoured them. They have time. No hurry. They have three days ahead of them. Sixty-four hours.

I'll hold out, Michael told himself. Don't worry about a thing, friend. You won't be betrayed by me *or* my legs. Maybe I'll lose them. But a pair of legs for a friend's life is not expensive.

Michael sees himself smiling at his own thoughts: to imagine that there was a time when he thought he could save all of mankind by the suffering he took upon himself! Then it was not one human life that he wanted to save, but human life itself. Not one man, but man. But he had lost those ideas somewhere along the way. He no longer has the heart he had then. All he has now is legs, and it is precisely they, his legs, the legs he never thought twice about, that are called upon now to save a friend's life.

Twelve years ago. He opens the door to the little room where they are waiting for him: Kalman, the yellow-bearded master, and his fellow students Hersh-Leib and Menashe.

"Master," he calls out, "I have returned from far away. I have something to tell you. Something you don't know. Listen to me! It's important!"

The master closes the book, but his hands remain on its black cover. Hersh-Leib and Menashe do the same.

"I ran," Michael says. "I've run eleven or twelve years. Not stopping once. I've traveled through time and space to share my discovery with you."

Hands clenched on the book, head bowed, the master says, "Speak."

In a breathless staccato, Michael tells them briefly of his experience. "The legs," he says. "We never thought they were important. We were wrong. They too can save lives. Not many, of course. But a few. Isn't just one enough?"

His words fall into a hostile, glacial silence. Michael was expecting an explosion of joy, then compliments and thanks.

"Too late," the master says. "You've come too late."

"How can that be—too late?" Michael cries.

The master is silent. Then, moved by a frightful foreboding, Michael stoops and peers beneath the table. And he understands. Neither the master nor his disciples have legs. Instead they have columns of gnarled wood. Michael chokes back a shriek of terror.

"You've come too late," the master says. "What you were going to tell us, we already know. This world can no longer be saved by the head or the heart. No one can do anything about that. Each generation has the savior it deserves. Ours deserves legs. Tomorrow's will not have even that. It will perhaps be saved by earthworms or squids or wild beasts, who knows?"

"That strike you as pretty, a man with two columns of knotty wood for legs?" asked the officer between two yawns.

Very low, the words not escaping his throat, Michael answered, "Yes, it does. There's nothing prettier, nothing more rare, than a man with legs of wood. Kalman, Hersh-Leib, Menashe: their calm, brooding beauty has no equal among mortals. To be like them would be an honor, a distinction, a claim to manhood."

Kalman, Hersh-Leib, Menashe, where are you? How far did your legs carry you? To Auschwitz? Last stop. Everybody out. All the legs step out and are transmuted to wood, the better to be consumed. How many human lives have you saved? By how many years have you shortened the exile of the universe? Ah, what a spectacle! Legs burning, six legs burning, twelve million legs burning!

In Szerencseváros everybody thought they were mad. Kalman, with his yellowing beard and his

narrow hunched shoulders; Hersh-Leib, the shoemaker's son, who scratched his nose whenever he
struggled with a difficult passage of the Talmud; Menashe, the shy orphan taken in by a rich family, who
gave everything he received to the poor.

They're mad, they said in Szerencseváros, the city
that had the luck to see them born and grow up. Kalman, people said, is a mad teacher who teaches his
mad disciples a life of folly and the folly of life. He is
a teacher who renounces reason at the start in order
to find it later, embellished and vigorous, at the heart
of madness.

Kalman is dangerous, the people repeated. And
they came to plead with Michael's father: don't en-
trust your only son to him! He'll destroy him for you!
You'll lose him!

But Michael insisted. He was thirteen. He had just
been *bar mizvah*, privileged to have the Borsher rabbi
tie the knots of his *Tephillin-shel-yad* the first time he
put them on. Varady and Milika: forgotten, repulsed.
Latin, mathematics and physics: abandoned. Only
God existed. And only Kalman knew how one could
be united with him.

The year that he spent beside the master was for
Michael the most wondrous of his life. The most profound, the fullest. Suddenly all actions had meaning,
occupied a definite place in that immense mosaic of
which even the outlines escape our understanding.
God was *presence*. He manifested himself in every
thing, behind every act. An aspect of God was concealed even in evil, and the theory of the *Nitzotzot*
said so poetically: every man possesses a divine spark.
The Shekina is the sum of the sparks. Let the Shekina
—the divine emanation—be reunited with God, and
the world will have achieved its final liberation.

With Kalman studies began at six in the morning
and ended well after midnight. The first hours of the

morning were dedicated to the books of the *Mussar;* then came passages of the Talmud; at night they let themselves be carried away by the dazzling pages of the *Zohar,* the Book of Splendor, in which truth is given to a man like a woman who opens herself to a lover: in total abandon, blindly.

Michael had to defeat strenuous opposition from his father in order to join Kalman's disciples. "I don't like fanatics," his father said angrily. "They do not live; choosing eternity, they forget life, which is healthy, simple, and joyful; which is made up of laughter and stupidities and daily hopes and childish illusions, of adventures that fear no tomorrow!"

But the boy won his mother over. She knew Kalman's reputation; people were afraid of him, certainly, but they admired him. And she hoped that the admiration would also be reflected upon her son. In people's eyes, to be a disciple of the yellow-bearded master was the equivalent of a title. "God gave me a son," she said; "He will be proud of him."

That year Michael led a life in no way normal. His father had seen truly. The boy spent only brief moments at home. He ate little, slept little, spoke little. All winter long he fasted on Mondays and Thursdays. Saturdays he opened his lips only to pray. The reason: silence purifies the mouth. He developed a taste for asceticism. In mortifying the flesh he hoped to increase the power of the spirit. He went so far as to leave his bed early in the morning and go out to roll in the snow stark naked. He took icy baths. He grew thinner, wasting away visibly. The wall he had erected between himself and the others grew higher and thicker.

His father suffered atrociously from all this. Once he waited up for his son until two in the morning. He bade the boy sit before him and asked, "Why do you go on making yourself sick?"

"My body offends me, father," Michael answered simply.

His father sighed. In resigned tones he told the boy the truth: "It offends you because you treat it as an enemy, which it is not. It is a gift of God every bit as much as the soul. God reveals or hides himself as well in the one as in the other. In the body he reveals himself visibly: why do you strike out against it? If the soul is the link between you and God, the body is the same between you and your fellows. Why destroy it? To kill the body, to remove a possibility of union between one human being and another, is as grave as destroying life. God is God because he is a bond between things and beings, between heart and soul, between good and evil, between the past and the future. To resemble God means to make perfect our own bond, to broaden it, render it more true, most useful, more radiant. Who does not live for man—for the man of today, for him who walks beside you and whom you can see, touch, love and hate—creates for himself a false image of God."

But he was arguing with the deaf. Michael was barely listening. He did not read the pain in his father's face.

Kalman and his three disciples held themselves outside Time. The planet was crumbling away, but they paid no attention. Stalingrad, Tobruk, El Alamein: they had never heard of those places. War was ravaging Europe, whole cities were disappearing overnight, whole peoples were dying in shame, others were rising in anger, the corpses were piling up, millions of men thought only of killing other millions of men, an enormous machine was grinding and roasting ten thousand Jews a day, ten thousand Jews a day, systematically, following an efficiently conceived program, the angel of death reigned, all-knowing master of all—but the ears of Kalman, Hersh-Leib, Menashe, and Michael remained closed to these rumblings of history. Withdrawn into their books, burrowing to the depths of their own essence, they were trying to follow Time to its ultimate source.

One day in the vestibule of the synagogue Michael heard a stranger chant a prayer that stunned him: "O God, be with me when I have need of you, but above all do not leave me when I deny you."

Michael reported the prayer to his master, and the latter cried, in a transport, "Ah, how beautiful! How beautiful! I want you to repeat it for me."

"'Oh God, be with me when I have need of you, but above all do not leave me when I deny you.'"

"Again, again!" Kalman cried, glowing.

"'Oh God, be with me . . .'" Michael had to repeat it five or six times.

Later, at twilight, between the prayer of *Minhah* and the prayer of *Maariv*, he found an opportunity to question his master. "That prayer—why is it so extraordinary?"

Kalman dropped an affectionate hand to the boy's shoulder. "Every man has a prayer that belongs to him, as he has a soul that belongs to him. And just as it is difficult for a man to find his soul, so it is difficult for him to find his prayer. Most people live with souls, and say prayers, that are not their own. Today, Michael, you found your prayer."

"And my soul?" the disciple asked, deeply moved. "The soul within me: is it my own?"

"Question it," said the master.

In the weeks that followed Michael could think of nothing else: what is this soul which I bear within me? Whose is it? And where is mine? In what body does it linger? Who am I? What am I? And most of all: where am I? Can I be living in a dream, in error, at a false address? Can it be that I am someone else?

He often contemplated his two colleagues and wondered if they had already solved the problem. Doubt-less they had. Older than he, Hersh-Leib, scratching his nose more and more, and Menashe, already quite wrinkled, were busy with other questions, other aspirations.

Hersh-Leib and Menashe came with him every Saturday to the *Bein-Hashmashot* meal at the home of the Borsher rabbi across the street. This is the most beautiful and the saddest of the Sabbath services. It takes place at twilight, at the hour that separates the "two suns." An obscurity at once unnerving and exalting reigns in the little synagogue. It is the hour when the sun, the star of day, has already vanished and the evening star has not appeared. Presiding over a long, narrow table, the rabbi sings in a muted murmur. They do not see him. Even his beard, snow-white, has melted into the darkness. The shadows of the Hasidim sway against the walls; their voices accompany the rabbi's but do not drown it out. The chants are distant, remote, of a delicate and pure melancholy. The Sabbath is slipping away, and they do not want to let it go. They seek a way to hold it back, to make it last. For the Sabbath is different from the other days. Composed of joys and fullnesses, it offers peace to the tormented and hope to hearts weary of hoping. The days of the week consist only of waiting. When the Messiah comes, all the days of the week will dissolve away, and only the Sabbath will remain. That is why the rabbi's chant is so sad, his voice broken. The Sabbath is slipping away, and that means that this week, too, the Messiah will not come.

It was during one of those *Bein-Hashmashot* services that Michael learned what he wanted to know.

"Some day," Hersh-Leib said suddenly, "I'll be strong enough to hold back the Sabbath."

"That's dangerous," Menashe said. "It's dangerous to want to rush things, to hurry the end. The world may not be ripe yet. We must wait for a sign, a sign."

Their fragile, almost transparent shadows swayed across the shadows of the Hasidim, to the rhythm of the chant which accompanied the Sabbath to its journey of six days and bade it farewell: farewell, Sabbath, come again quickly, as soon as you can, even sooner.

"You have to try," Hersh-Leib burst forth. "You have to try because . . ." He broke off; sobs shook him; he was choking. "You have to . . . you have to try . . . because . . . I can't go on!" He buried his face in his feverish hands and repeated endlessly the same words: "I can't go on. . . . I can't go on. . . ."

Hersh-Leib, the shoemaker's son, was the first of the three students to lose his mind. It happened a few weeks after the outburst in the synagogue. His father, a large man with broad shoulders, appeared before Kalman one morning and raised a great row. Hersh-Leib had left the house a bit before midnight. They had found him unconscious near the old synagogue.

Kalman went to see his pupil immediately. He ordered the parents and other relatives to clear out of the room and to leave him alone with the sick boy. A few hours later he went away without a word.

Hersh-Leib never left his bed again. He seemed totally paralyzed. His wide, staring eyes testified that there was nothing more to see; his sealed lips testified that there was nothing more to say. A strange apathy had consumed him. For hours on end he did nothing but stare straight ahead, into the void, almost without blinking. His father wailed ceaselessly: "I don't want him taken to the asylum. I don't want my son locked away. . . ."

Kalman is crazy and he passes the insanity to his students, said the good people of Szerencseváros. And friends came once more to plead with Michael's father: "Save him, save him while there's still time!"

Another conversation took place between father and son.

"You aren't afraid, Michael?"

"No, Father."

"I am."

"Don't be. I'm stronger than Hersh-Leib."

Less than three months later it was Menashe's turn to plunge into madness. They locked him up. The city was staggered. No one talked, no one argued about anything else. Kalman is mad, people cried in front of their houses, in the synagogue, at the market.

"Well, Michael?" asked his father.

"I'm not afraid."

"But, my son! Your mother and I can't sleep! We live in terror!"

"Don't worry, Father. Nothing will happen to me."

Nothing did: Michael did not follow his two comrades. The Germans saved him. They occupied Szerencseváros shortly after that, and all life as it had been ceased. The schools were closed, the synagogues shut tight. Michael left his master.

"Yes, Pedro," I said. "They were mad. In those years, nineteen forty-three, nineteen forty-four, you had to be crazy to believe that man has any control over his fate. You had to be crazy to hope for a victory of the spirit over the forces of evil, to imagine any possibility of redemption, of consolation; you had to have lost your reason, or sacrificed it, to believe in God, to believe in man, to believe in a reconciliation between them. Yes. They were mad. Out of their minds. Raving mad."

Pedro puffed at his pipe, took a few steps, came back to stand in front of me. "What became of them?"

"Wood," I said. "They turned into wood. When I saw them for the last time they were on their way to death. The madmen were the first to go. Kalman

walked in front, as if he were guiding them: he was the master. Hersh-Leib and Menashe—they'd taken him out of the asylum—followed on stretchers. That same night they rode into the sky on flames that fed the grief of a whole people. You're my friend, Pedro. Can you imagine what it was like?"

His face taut, almost incandescent, Pedro paced again. He couldn't stand still. He would have liked to do something. But what? God Himself has power only over the future. The past escapes Him.

Suddenly he stopped in front of me and shouted his anger to my face: "I don't like your prayer! It's humiliating! It gives God what he doesn't deserve: unconditional allegiance. I have a personal prayer, too, made just for me. This one: 'Oh God, give me the strength to sin against you, to oppose your will! Give me the strength to deny you, reject you, imprison you, ridicule you!' That's my prayer."

"I like it," I said. "It's a madman's prayer."

Pedro clenched his fists. Then he opened his hands and set them on my shoulders: "One more question, Michael. Is that why your city pulls at you so strongly? Do you want to see if Kalman left his madness behind, so you can take it upon yourself?"

I shook my head sadly. "No, Pedro. It has nothing to do with my master and his madness. With mine, maybe. But don't ask me any more. I'm cold."

At just that moment the officer tapped me on the shoulder. "Changing the guard! To the bathroom! Can you still walk? Yes? Don't be so happy about it. Not yet. It's too soon. Wait till tomorrow!"

Michael felt as though he were raising a great dead weight at each step. But he managed to keep his head high, as if that proved anything.

Second Prayer

SOMEONE HAD KNOCKED AT THE DOOR. AT FIRST TIMIDLY, then more firmly, insistently.

"What is it?" Michael called. As if he didn't know! Back again! He swore to seize my shadow, steal my sleep; he's appropriated my image and now he thinks I belong to him!

"I want to see you, talk to you, sit with you! I'm your brother, you said so yourself, and I need you, Michael!"

"Get out! Get out, Yankel, and don't come back! I've nothing to tell you and nothing to give you!"

The little imbecile! Surviving all that just to be run down by a truck! Couldn't watch his step, could he? Cross at the corner like everybody else? Maybe he did it deliberately, for my sake. So I won't be afraid any more, or ashamed. Won't want to smash my head against a wall in the darkness. I suppose I could ask him, Michael thought. I could open the door and tell him, "All right, come in. But on one condition: tell me whether you wanted to die." Yankel would agree. All he wanted was a chance to talk. But there it was: He'd never stop talking again. When the dead start talking, nothing can stop them. All you can do is rip off your ears, find some way to disappear. "Get out of here, Yankel! Get away from my door. Get out!"

"Why should you send me away? What have I done? I was your friend. I was there. I was with you when the night was darkest. Remember that?"

"Yes. But I don't want to remember it. I don't want you to remember it."

"Are you afraid?"

"Yes, I'm afraid. I'm afraid of you; of the bit of me that's part of you."

He hadn't opened the door. Silence. A pause. Is Yankel still there? Yes. Is he gone? Yes. He is there and he is not there. From now on there will be not one Yankel but a thousand, ten thousand. Someday they'll make up their minds to break down the door and cut me to ribbons. And no one will know why.

Michael arrived in Paris an adolescent and there became a man. For the first year he lived alone in a small room near the Hôtel de Ville. An uncle, a millionaire in New York, sent him ten dollars a month, and that was sufficient for rent, laundry, and bread. Ten dollars, five thousand francs on the black market, was a fortune in postwar France.

He knew not a living soul in Paris. He had no circle of friends, tied himself to no group, never received visits. His landlady made fun of him, his neighbors stared curiously at him, the baker knew that it was best to hand him a baguette every other day without the usual "How goes it?"

To keep from stumbling he needed much solitude, silence, and concentration. He was seeking his God, tracking him down. He would find Him yet. And then He won't get off as lightly as He did with Job. He won't win out so quickly. I'll be a match for Him. I'm not afraid of Him, not intimidated.

Michael never ceased resenting Job. That Biblical rebel should never have given in. At the last moment he should have reared up, shaken a fist, and with a resounding bellow defied that transcendent, inhuman Justice in which suffering has no weight in the balance.

I won't be had so easily, Michael thought. I'll ask him. Why do You play hide-and-seek with Your own image? You'll tell me that You created man in order to put him to the test—which explains nothing. The contest is too unequal; and anyway it isn't an explanation I need, but a clear, concise answer in human terms!

During the war Michael had seen saints become criminal, all for a crust of bread—a small, dry, filthy crust of bread. So that crust could change the natural order, could reverse the structure of creation! So that crust was enough to undo what the Almighty in His wisdom had done! Let's grant that the crust was, at the time, only obeying God, only transmitting God's will. But why? Why those sensational dramatics, those theatrical metamorphoses? To teach men that Jacob's ladder still awaits? That every being is a battlefield where two forces fight a hopeless war over an issue that he cannot understand? Is that it, and that alone, the meaning of our journey on this cursed earth? I want to know! Someone has to tell me!

Michael spent the whole year pursuing God grimly. He spent sleepless nights questioning himself, listening to the wisdom of the ancients; perhaps they knew. I'll follow Him, he thought. I'll follow Him everywhere, in time and in the universe. He won't get away; I'll stay on His trail whatever happens, whether He likes it or not. He took my childhood; I have a right to ask Him what He did with it.

Once decided to go the whole way, he never veered from the course he had set. He thought of nothing else. Not even of his vanished family. Above all, not of them. I will have all my life to remember, he told himself. For now, it was more important that he understand, that he forge a certainty. If God did not exist, it was necessary to announce it to the old man in the forest.

Savagely he contemplated himself. His burning glance searched the recesses of his being. Where is He? Where is He hiding? In my eyes, in my belly, in my mouth? Like a baby, Michael spent his days discovering his own body.

A pallid boy was the only one to come now and then, mainly on Thursdays, and knock at his bolted door. He was only twelve or thirteen, but his shoulders were already stooped. "Let me come in, Michael," he begged. "It's me. Do you recognize my voice?"

"I recognize your voice. But I don't want to see you. Understand me: I need to be alone. I need all my strength to finish my work. I can't see you or anybody. Get away!"

Yankel. The little prince. His nickname in the dark past. He wasn't a bad boy, not really. He had committed evil, but without realizing it. He was too young, too naïve to make of evil a way of life. The proof: at the liberation, the prisoners hadn't bothered him. They had arrested all the trusties, but left the boy alone even though he was one of them. They said: it isn't his fault; his wickedness is a deferred suffering. Poor boy, he'll suffer all the longer!

"I've got to talk to you, Michael. *Back there*, remember, you wanted to talk to me, all right!"

"Back there, yes. Here, no. I have no right. Not now. Afterward I'll talk to you again. When I've finished. Be patient, Yankel! Go back to school!"

When he arrived in France Yankel had been welcomed by a relief committee and placed in an elementary school where, of course, he was altogether out of place. The oldest, the terror of his class, he refused to fit himself in. He did not know how to read or write or to speak any one language correctly. To be seated among kids much younger than himself infuriated him. In a mixture of Yiddish, Polish, and German he incessantly insulted the teacher, who had no idea how to tame him.

During the two years he had spent *back there* he had learned all that anyone could learn about men and their real nature—all, if not more. Why had the Germans spared him, while a million Jewish children had been reduced to ashes? Inexplicable mystery.

In the camp where Michael had known him he was the *Piepel*, the spoiled child of those in charge. For them he was evidence that somewhere in the world, beyond the barbed wires and the savage shouts, there was still something like childhood.

Well fed and warmly dressed, the little prince strolled among the barracks, inspiring envy, fear, pity. He possessed the power of life and death over those adults who never saw him without recalling their own children, whom the winds had dispersed. He gave them orders, he, the urchin, and they hastened to obey. They feared his anger, for it was like that of those in command. Once he had slapped a prisoner whose sickly appearance displeased him. The man had fallen to his knees. "Get up!" the little prince had ordered. "It was just for fun." The man obeyed. Appeased, Yankel drew a chunk of bread from his pocket and offered it to the man. "Thank you," he murmured. "Thank you very much. I know it was just for fun."

No one felt hatred toward him. Rather a kind of pity. They thought, "Poor child, they're killing his heart, poisoning his soul. He's too young to resist. He doesn't even know he ought to resist. Poor child. At least the rest of us had our childhood. Not he."

Yankel was not evil, though he often displayed cruelty. Children are like that. They inflict pain because they don't know, not yet, the significance of suffering. He was only playing. Those old men who fell silent at his approach, who abased themselves before him, who cowered in his presence: they amused him. He never wanted to do them harm, not really. He simply wanted to see them become humble, defenseless children. Afterward, he always made it up to them.

One day Michael came to him: "You've got to save my father. They put him on the list for deportation. You're the only one who can get his name crossed off."

The little prince spoke in wide-eyed astonishment: "You too? You need me too? I thought only the grownups had favors to ask."

"I'm a grownup," Michael said.

"How old are you?"

"That's not important. Here you get old fast. We're too close to death. Being close to death is what makes you old."

"You're lying! You're trying to scare me! I'm not old! I'll never get old!"

"Don't be angry. Everybody gets old."

"Not me! You hear? Not me. And I want you to tell me so! Otherwise I won't do anything for your father."

Michael's face darkened. "It was only a joke, little prince. You'll never get old. Not you."

Michael's father was not deported that time. Afterward a strange friendship bound the two young prisoners. When the transport guards were gone Yankel came often to chat with Michael. He brought bread, soup; Michael passed them on to his father.

"You love him that much?"

"Yes. That much. And more."

"What do you do to love someone?"

"You don't do anything. You just love."

"You're lucky. I'd like to love, too."

Yankel's father had been killed on the very day they evacuated the ghetto: a soldier shot him in the back of the neck. Just like that. Without a reason, without anger, without even blinking or changing expression. He holstered his Mauser, glanced vaguely at the still-twitching corpse, and strolled off to chat with a buddy farther along. Michael was luckier. His father died on a mattress of rotten straw shortly before the liberation.

"Open up, Michael! Open up!"

"Get out of here, Yankel! I need to be alone."

Yankel had been there, close by. Father was dying, his face darkening as Michael watched him. But Yankel was not watching the old man. He studied me, Michael thought. And he had never forgiven the boy for that.

One day the uncle in New York cut off his monthly money. He was angry, the uncle: his burst of charity was over. The Manhattan millionaire expected somewhat more gratitude from his nephew, somewhat more effusive letters, somewhat warmer thanks. But Michael had never quite learned to translate gratitude into words, written or spoken. His uncle saw in that a sign of ingratitude, and consequently notified him that he would do well to equip himself as soon as possible with another uncle. Michael had no other uncle at hand.

Hunger never bothered him excessively. He believed himself strong enough to resist it. From the days with Kalman he had mastered the useful art of dominating his body: to eat became a thing of no importance. He did not enjoy meals; he took them reluctantly. So the thought that soon he would not have the price of a piece of bread did not trouble him. Of God, he demanded other things than daily bread.

On the other hand, he worried about the rent. Nine hundred francs a month. It is easier to fight one's stomach than one's landlady. She would not hesitate to evict her "little priest."

That evening Michael betook himself to the synagogue near the Faubourg Montmartre, much frequented, he knew, by refugees from central Europe. He had to find money, work, as quickly as possible. They would know where and how.

His heart pounding, he opened the wooden door. Since Szerencseváros he had not set foot in a sacred place. An indefinable fear gripped him. What would he find inside? Perhaps his dreams, the yearning chants of the Rabbi of Borshe, or Kalman's silent, ecstatic meditations.

The synagogue was almost empty. Hardly a *minyan* of the faithful. They were preparing to recite the prayer of *Maariv;* the prayer of *Minha* was over. They were chatting. Politics, finances, the situation in Palestine. Michael felt a wrench at his heart. He remembered the synagogue of his childhood, where external realities had no place.

A man broke away from the group and came toward him: "*Sholem aleichem,*" he said, extending his hand.

"*Aleichem sholem.*"

"Where are you from?"

"Hungary. Szerencseváros."

"Really? What's your name?"

Michael told him. The man cried joyfully that he had known Michael's father. Yes, he was from Hungary too. He had occasionally visited Szerencseváros. He knew many people there. The Goldblatts, the

Schreibers, the Fuchses. "I knew your father. A man of rare intelligence. He's dead?"

"He's dead," Michael answered.

The tone of the question, like that of the answer, was detached, cold, impersonal. After the war people asked "Your father is dead?" as they would have asked "Your father's in textiles?" And you answered "Yes, my father is dead" as you would have answered "Yes, my father's in textiles."

Michael asked about ways to find work, to make money. The man, thin of face and piercing of eye, painted a gloomy picture for the boy: "Did you just drop from the moon? Don't you know what things are like in France?"

In France, he explained, the law on refugees is made for millionaires. France is happy to be the home of the stateless, on condition that they be rolling in money. A refugee without resources suffers the fate of the marginal man, the second-class citizen. The concierge, the grocer, the police sergeant, above all the police sergeant, are all his superiors, judges of his right to live. To have his resident's permit extended the refugee must first prove that he is not working; second, that he has means of support. How can a man supply his needs without the right to earn a living? No questions. The sergeant asks the questions.

Nevertheless, the man with piercing eyes gave him the address of a committee of aid to refugees. Michael called upon them the next morning. After waiting in line for three hours he was received by a morose bureaucrat who subjected him to a detailed interrogation. Why had he come to France? Why had he no money? Yes, why? How long did he propose to live in Paris at the expense of society? Several times Michael wanted to up-end the table and slam the door behind him. But he restrained his anger, that scornful anger of the humiliated.

Finally he received a few thousand francs. "I'll pay you back," he said.

"All right, all right," said the bureaucrat, impatient, dry. "We know that tune. Go on."

When he got home Michael went to see the landlady and paid her six months' rent in advance. "What!" she exclaimed, flabbergasted. "Where did you get so much money? I hope you didn't do anything stupid."

"Don't worry. 'Little priests' have connections Up There, you know."

He passed a night of nervous agitation, punctuated by dreams. He awoke with a start, panting, fury in his heart. He got up well before dawn and paced his room. For the first time in his life he felt hunted, persecuted. There was something behind the door, he was sure of it. Someone was spying on him. Someone had it in for him. Where could he flee, he wondered. Sleep was no longer a refuge.

The next morning he enrolled at the Sorbonne, not to study but to acquire the status of a student, which would qualify him for temporary employment. He had only three thousand francs left; he had to find work before it dribbled away. He was sent to give Hebrew lessons at the home of an industrialist named Weiler.

"It's for my son," the industrialist told him, a distinguished man with graying hair. "He's seven years old. He knows nothing of Judaism. He doesn't even know how to read the Bible. I can offer you two hundred francs per lesson; will that do?"

"Perfectly, sir."

After the third lesson Monsieur Weiler informed Michael that they could do without his services. With some reason. Accustomed to speaking to children as though they were already adults, Michael was sowing seeds of confusion in the boy's soul. He had asked him to read the first verse of Genesis: *Breishit bara elohim et hashamaim veet haaretz*. In the beginning God created the heaven and the earth.

"Why?" Michael asked.

"I don't know what you mean," the boy complained in total confusion.

"Why did God create heaven and earth?"

"I don't know, sir."

"Doesn't the question interest you?"

At that moment the door to the drawing room opened and the elder Weiler entered with the haughty dignity of a butler. He ordered his son to go to his room and turned to the imbecile tutor: "The question does interest me. Perhaps you know the answer?"

"No, sir," Michael said, embarrassed.

Weiler proffered a thousand-franc note. "Keep it. We won't need you any longer."

Michael, proud and stupid, refused the bill. And Weiler did not insist. He gave him six hundred francs. "You are too proud, young man," he said.

"That's possible."

"I don't mean about the money."

"All the better." Michael hastened to take his leave.

Home again, he found a brief note under his door: "I looked for you. May I see you at last? I need your help. Yankel." No, Michael thought. Not yet. The time isn't ripe. Right now I have to create a new skin for myself, a new life.

He returned to the employment bureau, which insisted absolutely that he make a career of teaching Hebrew: they found him a job at a children's home. He gave one lesson there. The thirty pupils never gave him a chance to open his mouth. They clattered and racketed as if they had decided beforehand to deafen him. The directress—who was, of course, not far off—explained it to him when the hour was over: "This is no job for you, young man. You are too humble with children. That's bad, not pedagogical. Children admire pride, and fear it. I speak from experience. They aren't afraid of you, so they won't admire you. You're too good, too humble, for that pack of savages."

Having pocketed the two hundred francs Michael went home, his heart bitter, determined never to try again. Preaching from the height of her experience, the directress was right: it was no work for him. He was, it seemed, too humble and too proud.

So he looked for something else. With no great success. To be a porter at Les Halles, or a messenger, is a privilege reserved exclusively to citizens of the great French Republic.

And then, on the street near the Opéra, he met a childhood friend. Meir seemed prosperous. Elegantly turned out, he was living at the Grand Hotel; he had taken on the manner of a successful movie actor and radiated prosperity. "What a pleasure to run into you," Meir said, "after so many years!"

"I'm happy to see you, too. What are you doing in Paris?"

"Business trip. I come here often, you know. A lot of people to see, all highly placed, very important."

"What kind of business are you in?"

"Import-export."

The English phrase veiled a simple, and less prestigious, activity. Meir was simply a smuggler, though his range was wide.

"Aren't you ashamed?" Michael asked naïvely.

"Ashamed?" Meir echoed, cut to the quick.

"Yes, ashamed. Ashamed of lying, of living outside the law, of doing illegal things, you know."

Meir extracted the cigarette from a corner of his

mouth and ground it out beneath his heel. "Listen, my friend. You're a dreamer. You're still living in the past. Not me. Not for me the good old days and all those fancy ideas, and the laws, and the principles, and the ideals, and the fine words, the pompous phrases—to hell with that. We live in a jungle. You adapt or you die. I don't want to die, so I adapt. Dog bites man or man bites dog, that was all right in Szerencseváros. Here and now, wherever you look it's man biting man. I act accordingly. I refuse to let myself be bitten. I have weapons and I use them. Look around you. Ask any passer-by how he's doing. The most common answer is, 'I make out.' Well, I'll tell you: I don't just make out, I make *it*. I don't defend; I attack."

Dumbfounded, Michael listened. They had been childhood friends. Meir too went to the Rabbi of Borshe to pray, to chant, to absorb the presence of the holy elder. How long ago that was!

"I don't recognize you, Meir."

"I've changed, the times have changed, you too, you've changed."

"But . . . what you do is dishonest!"

"You say so, do you?" Meir cried, swelling in exasperation. "You dare to invoke principle? But who *is* honest these days! You think anyone who's survived the war could have stayed honest? The honest men are all dead! Murdered or suicides. The others—including you and me—are whatever you like, except honest. They compromise. They make a deal with memory, with the past, with their suffering. They act as if nothing had happened, as if the war was only a parenthesis they can open and close whenever they want to. Is that honest? Isn't it rather hypocrisy, treason—and of the worst kind at that? Have they got any right to betray the dead—the dead, who can't even defend themselves?"

"Wrong," Michael said dreamily. "They defend themselves very well. Sometimes they even get tired of defending, and then they attack."

Meir stared in astonishment. "What are you talking about?"

"Nothing, Meir, nothing. I didn't say a word."

They spent the evening together in conversation, reliving memories of childhood, comparing their worldly fates. When he understood his friend's desperate position Meir very kindly proposed that Michael join him: "I'm at the head of a large organization that covers Europe and extends into Asia and Africa. If it appeals to you . . ."

If Michael had small aptitude for teaching, he had still less for smuggling. Meir lost no time discovering that. They took a trip to Belgium together. They were to bring back diamonds. On the way up Michael betrayed such terror when the customs agent asked him, "Anything to declare?" that Meir decided on the spot to send him back the next day, alone and without "baggage."

"But what were you afraid of, for God's sake?" he protested when they were across the border. "You didn't have anything illegal with you!"

"I'm sorry," Michael said hoarsely. "I got the feeling that he was reading my thoughts, that he knew why we were making the trip."

Meir shrugged, discouraged. "What you're saying is stupid. They're customs men, not fortunetellers."

"I'm terribly sorry. . . ."

"Oh, drop it! You're a hopeless case. With ideas like that, with that kind of inhibitions, you won't go far in life, believe me."

Michael went back the next day. At the frontier, when the customs agent asked him what he had to declare, Michael smiled happily and answered in proud, ringing tones, "Nothing, sir. Nothing at all!"

Of course that made him suspect in the eyes of the shrewd agent, who escorted him to an unoccupied compartment where he searched him from head to foot in accordance with the regulations.

Not long afterward—more precisely, on the following Thursday, during the week of the High Holidays —Yankel knocked at his door.

"You've come out of your solitude," he called. "I know you have. I came by several times and you weren't in your room. You have no more excuse for refusing to see me."

Michael stiffened and did not answer. He realized suddenly that his room was really too small, a stuffy hole: only walls and an opaque, paralyzing silence. I'll have to move, he thought. Leave this room. A shame the rent's paid in advance.

"I know you're there," Yankel said. "I heard you walking around."

"What do you want with me, Yankel? Why don't you leave me in peace? Go on. Go away."

"I want to see you and talk to you and tell you what I'm doing and how I'm doing. You know I have nobody in Paris except you."

"Don't you have any friends at school?"

"No. They're too little, too happy; they don't interest me. They bore me. Can *you* see me playing with them, in the schoolyard or in the street?"

The little prince: he had reigned over a kingdom of old men, had imposed his law, his moods, his will upon them. He had spoken to them as a master, conscious of his superiority, of his absolute powers. One word from him announced hope or the death of hope. His power illustrated the grotesque side of the situation: thousands of men trembled before an urchin playing games. True, Michael thought: I can't very

well see him playing with children in the schoolyard
or the street.

"Let me in, Michael. I promise not to stay long."

"Why do you want to see me so much?"

"You're the only person who can understand me.
You're the only one who knows that I'm not a child,
and can't be one."

Michael took his head between his hands and
squeezed hard, very hard. He squeezed until it hurt,
and experienced an unwonted satisfaction. I lose all
the battles, he thought. What does it matter, one defeat more or less? He went to open the door, but at
the last moment yielded to a sudden surge of will:
"Another time, Yankel. A little later on. I'll listen, but
not now. You can't understand. It's not easy. I ask you
to have faith in me."

He spoke in the cracked tones of a man who knows
himself in danger.

*   *   *

The following months only aggravated Michael's
material problems. Once he had spent the money
given him by the refugee committee, he began to
know real hunger. Some weeks he did without a hot
meal altogether. He spent whole days walking about
with an empty belly. Those days he returned in
shame to the synagogue and borrowed a few hundred
francs from the man who had known his father, to
buy bread and a cup of coffee with real milk.

Autumn had come. Fleeing his haunted room, Michael discovered the beauty of Paris: under a copper
sun the city was bathed in an antique yellow glow.
Only the horizon suggested any blue. Paris in the fall
is more handsome, more sober, than in spring. As if
the city were allowing itself, in some apprehension, to
be swept along toward winter, but offering a passive,

feminine resistance. It is that resistance which gives it
its solemn, ripe beauty.

That year Paris was in the throes of what seemed
to be a philosophico-political struggle with its conscience. The war, the massacres in Europe, Hiro-
shima, all lacerated men's memories. Young people,
tumbling into a world created by their elders, into a
system established in advance, were trying to understand, to grasp the incomprehensible. Everybody
talked existentialism, everybody discussed Commu-
nism, everybody fought about the word "realism."
The password was commitment. It was no longer necessary to accept, or to accept oneself. Man is what he
rejects—they said—and what he chooses, and what he
does. The deep thinkers defined man at random and
placed him everywhere at once, on the left, on the
right, above, below. Everybody talked about dignity,
liberty, action. You have to act—they said—and you have
to fight, you have to shout, you have to say no. Despair—
they said—stands guard at every exit, hell is the neighbor who snores all night, the absurd has usurped the
throne abdicated by God, therefore you have to *do*
something! A gesture, an action, a revolution, on the
personal or the universal level, what difference did it
make? God is dead, and only the false messiahs, the
false prophets, knew it. And no one shouts louder, no
one makes himself more clearly understood than a false
prophet announcing the arrival of a false messiah. So
Paris, that year, had become an echo chamber in which
converged all the sounds and vibrations of those who
were afraid of silence (which they confused with
emptiness), who were afraid of fear (which they took
for cowardice), and who chatted only to reassure
themselves.

Michael followed that revolution in philosophical
thought from a considerable distance and in a very

detached manner. He was hungry, and coffee with real milk was expensive at the Café Flore.

He walked a lot. Within a few weeks he had explored the most out-of-the-way corners of Paris. He discovered alleys that greeted the sun only at one rare moment each day, and lost it again immediately; places where the murmur of the Seine was sharper than elsewhere; deserted parks peopled only by old men dreaming of their youth with the help of yellowed photographs. He thought better while he walked; his ideas seemed clearer, more dynamic. Later he became Pedro's friend for the simple reason that Pedro knew how to walk; few people did. Michael came to the conclusion that the legs are as useful, as indispensable to awareness, as the eyes or the fingers. No one knows the earth who has not walked upon it. The primitive gesture of the conqueror, his boot pressing down on the enemy, means simply that he knows him, and therefore possesses him, is the master of his destiny. If all nations, in the long course of history, have taken bitter pains to trample on the Jews, it is perhaps because they wished to know that strange people who, more than any other, possess the secret of survival, the key to the mystery of time, the formula for endurance. Michael was hungry, but he went on walking and learning what he was: he seemed to be walking on himself. Sometimes he sank to a bench, exhausted, or collapsed on the white quais of the Seine. But his fatigue was not at all tainted by bitterness.

One day he found his counterpart. He was strolling the quais at an even, tranquil pace—the pace of a man headed nowhere—when a stranger approached and stopped him: "Wait, Monsieur," the other said in a low voice. "I'm hungry." And he extended an open hand, palm cupped, awaiting alms.

Petrified, Michael stared at him. There was something hard and desperate in the features of the un-shaved man, a shifty uneasiness in his eyes. Michael, who had not a penny, suddenly experienced so much sympathy, so total a comprehension of the man, that he broke into a smile. "Me too," he said. "I'm hungry too."

For an instant they stood motionless, jostled by passers-by, their eyes locked. Then the man grimaced vaguely and said, "It's a dog's life." He turned his back and was gone. Did he believe me? Michael wondered. Did he understand me?

Years later he found himself in Spain. A reporter, he had—relatively—enough money. He was visiting Barcelona. At night he loved to stroll alone on the Ramblas, where even the shadows flat against the walls had throbbing hearts and thirsty souls. He also liked adventuring in the narrow, dark alleyways where he could sense the presence of those too enfeebled to sleep.

It was about two in the morning. He emerged from an obscure byway that gave onto the boulevard, when a boy, almost an infant, in rags, popped up out of nowhere and stood before him, hand open: "*Señor, tengo hambre.*"

For a few seconds Michael, paralyzed by the shock of memory, was incapable of motion. His expression must have been frightening: the boy took sudden fear and ran off. Only then Michael snapped out of his trance and broke into a run, following the boy and shouting, "Come back! *Niño, ven!* I'll give you money! All I have! Don't be afraid, *niño!* I won't hurt you! Come back, *niño*, come back!"

But his cries in the night, while they roused curious onlookers, only added to the boy's fears. After a good ten minutes of pursuit, Michael lost sight of him. He gave up. Surrounded by passers-by who understood nothing of what had happened before their eyes, he sank to the sidewalk, his back against the wall of a house. It was as if he had lost his peace of mind, his soul. He wanted to weep.

But Michael loved those months of total penury. Fasting, he saw things and beings with often striking clarity. He entered the world of the *clochards,* a world barred to those who could eat at will. He made a few friends there. He accepted their bread, their wine, their incoherent confessions. They accepted his silences, he their frenzies, their grotesque joys. In the rue Mouffetard he felt at home. He was introduced to one of the seven "elders" who rule—no one knows how or since when—that disillusioned fraternity which permits its members to discard their identities. Michael understood that ceasing to be a man, by whatever means, and being one were equally difficult.

What does a *clochard* dream of when the night drops its alcoholic peace over him? What does he see in the morning mists when the only sound in the universe is that of the wind tumbling with the sky, rousing it, lashing it, as if to punish it, blow it into the Seine?

"Thirst," a ragged friend said, swimming in his own drool. "I dream that I'm thirsty. I dream the whole world's thirsty." One night that friend told a parable. A man is trudging across the desert. He is thirsty, intolerably thirsty. Not a drop of water. He walks with the sun and hopes to reach an oasis. He walks, bearing the beast beneath his skin: it eats him alive. Near the end of his tether, he sees mirages. He pictures himself drinking clear, cool, fresh water. Suddenly the world is bathed in water. The sky. The white sand. His own body. All transmuted to liquid. And he is happy, that man. He is no longer thirsty. And at that point he reaches the oasis. The palm tree, the spring. He drops to his knees, and like the first man ever he touches the calm surface with the tip of his tongue. And he leaps to his feet, furious and disappointed.

The *clochard* swigged at his wine and added, "I've drunk from that spring. I prefer thirst."

And Michael thought: who knows? Maybe these people, the *clochards,* are the true wise men of Europe, the yogis of the Western world. They aren't out to save the world or their own consciences: they don't give a damn. They've renounced not only the comfort of their bodies but also their dignity, the miserable dignity of mankind. Let anyone talk about sanity, truth, passion, reality, and they'll be the first to laugh.

Rosh Hashana. New Year's Day. A very familiar rapping at the door. He hasn't gone to synagogue either, Michael thought. Why should he? He never set foot inside a holy place in his life. And I? With all my might I keep myself from running to it. My legs ask only to help me bow down, my lips only to pray, my eyes only to weep. But I will not go! If God is God he deserves better than my weakness.

"It's me—Yankel. Open up. Please."

Michael started. And idea struck him: what better day for a confrontation than Rosh Hashana? It would pain him; so? On New Year's Day a man ought to feel pain. He rose from the table, heavily. He thought: this will be my way of falling to my knees to ask forgiveness. At the door he hesitated for an instant, as if listening for the beat of his own heart; then he turned the knob in a sudden, decided motion.

There he was: the little prince. It was their first meeting since the camp. Wearing a striped gray suit and a dark blue tie, Yankel seemed even younger, slimmer. His eyelids twitched: a tic. His eyes seemed long extinct.

"Come in."

Yankel hesitated, and then entered hastily. He sat

on the only chair as Michael flopped down on the bed. Uneasy, they were silent. Tension swelled in the room. Michael was jumpy, all his nerves exposed. This is the only person in the world who knows, he thought. He was right there, that close. He saw me. He saw me as I am, as I am when the skin is stripped away. I live in his mind. In his mind I'm immutable.

The little prince drew out a pack of cigarettes and offered them. Michael declined. Hoarsely, he asked a question; something had to be said to dissipate the awful silence. "You've begun to smoke? At your age?"

"At my age? I'm old, you know." He lit his cigarette; then, "Have I changed?"

Slowly Michael inspected him. I love him and I hate him, he thought. Why that love, why that hate? "Yes, you've changed. You're more worried. More tormented."

"Not you. You've stayed the same. Anybody would think you were still back there."

Michael blushed. He would have liked to ask, Do you remember Karl? Karl was a brute with a bull's head. You remember him, don't you? He liked you. Even he liked you. And yet he was a killer, a sick killer.

But he said nothing. Yankel would have answered, "Yes, I remember. Karl was a brute. I was a brute too." And he might have added, "Not you. You weren't a brute." And Michael had no wish to hear that. Michael did not want him to remember. One memory leads to another and the pit yawns wider with each.

"Tell me a little about yourself. What are you doing in school? Do you like your courses? Your schoolmates?"

Yankel sketched a pained smile and launched the story of his life in Paris. Michael tried hard, but could not follow the thread of it.

When the trouble with Karl occurred Michael's father was still alive. Karl had condemned an old man to twenty-five lashes for some minor negligence. The victim's friends came to beg the little prince to get him off. "He's too weak," they said. "He won't make it. He'll die before the tenth stroke." But that day Yankel had not been in the mood to play guardian angel. They came to Michael: "You're his friend. He'll listen to you." Michael failed like the others. "I can't do anything about it!" the little prince exclaimed angrily. "All the old man has to do is hold out!" Michael insisted, but his friend proved intractable. "You're turning into an animal!" Michael shouted, furious. "You'll be like Karl soon! You won't be able to feel kindness or pity!" Yankel stared at him, astounded. "And you?" he asked defiantly. "You consider yourself good, and just?" "Yes," Michael said. Yankel thought it over briefly and gave way to an evil smile: "I've got a proposition for you. You're stronger, tougher than the old man. You'd stand the twenty-five lashes better than he would. You wouldn't die. Do you want to try it in his place?" He's bluffing, Michael thought. He's testing me. He won't go through with it. "It's all right with me," he answered. Yankel went to see Karl, who found the idea funny. The flogging was to take place in public the next day, after the soup was passed around, in front of the barracks. Up to the last second Michael was convinced that it would never come to pass. The little prince isn't really bad, he told himself. He won't let Karl beat me. He was on his knees, doubled forward, his chest on the block, still thinking. It's a bluff! when the first slash of the bullwhip cut into him. There won't be a second, he thought. It came. Then the third. And the fourth. And the fifth too. Five strokes. Yankel was watching the performance. Michael had managed to keep his teeth clenched; no cry had escaped him. Now he waited for the rest in a sort of calm. Only the first few really hurt, he thought. Seven or twenty-five, it's all the same. But there was no sixth stroke. Yankel gestured to Karl: Stop. Karl said, "All right," and went back to the barracks, indifferent and bored. Yankel hurried to help his friend rise. "Are you badly hurt?" he asked. "Not at all," Michael answered. "Do you detest me?" "No," Michael said, wincing. "I know it was only a joke."

Did I hate him then? Michael wondered. No. I can remember it perfectly. I looked him straight in the eye and tried to smile. He was sinking under the weight of remorse and shame. He offered me bread, and a double pat of margarine. I accepted them and said to him, "Let it go, Yankel. Don't worry about it. You're still my little brother, like before." Anger was stirring in me, but not hate. It was only later on . . .

"That's why I had to see you," Yankel went on. "With you I feel comfortable, an old man in the company of another old man; a link to my past. But with the kids at school . . ."

Michael thought: Of course, that's it. I'm the only man alive over whom you still have power. The others aren't afraid of you now. But you still give me the shivers. Each of us has a ghost that follows him everywhere in this life. You are mine. Because of you I humble myself.

"You haven't answered," Yankel said.

"What'd you say?"

"I asked you a question."

"A question? What?"

"You weren't even listening!"

"Yes, Yankel. I was listening. I didn't hear everything, but I was listening."

"Then why don't you answer me? I asked why you wouldn't see me."

"I've told you over and over!" Michael answered, annoyed. "I needed solitude, meditation. I had a job of work to do, a question to settle, a battle to win. A man never gets through to things unless he's alone."

"Is that the only reason?"

Michael bowed his head involuntarily. Yankel was playing with a cigarette, inspecting it from one end to the other. Here I am bowing humbly, Michael told himself. He's still the little prince. I'm the only man on earth for whom he'll always be the little prince.

"I asked you something: is that the only reason you kept me away?"

"Of course it is," Michael said. "Of course. What makes you think there'd be another?"

"I don't know." A pause, and then: "I think you have a grudge against me."

Michael looked up suddenly and met the boy's anguished eyes; they blushed at the same time. He's drowning too, Michael thought. They won't let him go, release him to the world of the living. "Me? A grudge?" he cried without conviction. "How can you talk that way? After all the ordeals we went through together . . ." He stopped himself: I was about to say some stupid things. You, little prince, you kept your eyes open. ". . . How can you talk that way? After all you did for my father? Do you think I've forgotten that?"

Yankel left the question unanswered. Distraught, infinitely solemn, he drew in smoke, filled his lungs, exhaled in long bursts. To read his thoughts! Michael said to himself. To learn exactly what he knows, what he wants, what he's planning! All right, Yankel! I've given you a hand: talk! I've brought my father into the room; take him and use him against me! What are you waiting for?

"Do you remember Karl?" the boy asked very gently.

So that's it, Michael thought. He thinks I detest him because of Karl; and I think he detests me be-

cause of my father. He's using Karl as a counter-
weight; telling me, "You see? Every man has his own
burden." It was Michael's turn to leave the question
unanswered. "Tell me, Yankel, do you remember the
night my father died?"

The boy's gaunt features expressed astonishment.
He was still for a moment, gauging the situation, siz-
ing it up, and then: "Yes. Your father's last night. Barracks number fifty-seven. Third row of beds to the
left of the door. You were sitting on the edge of his
soiled mattress and you never took your eyes off him.
That was all you did: you watched him slip away.
His lips mumbled unintelligible words and you were
trying to catch them, to decode them with your eyes."

"What were you doing then?"

"I was crying," Yankel said with a smile.

That's true, Michael thought. You were crying. I
saw you weep silent tears. It was at that moment that
I began to love you like a brother. But I didn't cry.
There's the truth: I looked on and didn't cry. And you
saw it. And I can't forgive you that. "Yankel, what
was I doing while my father lay dying?"

"I just told you. Nothing. You didn't do anything.
You just watched."

"I didn't cry."

"No. You didn't cry."

"Did you wonder why I didn't cry when my father
was lying there and dying?"

"No."

"You're lying! You know you're lying!"

"I'm telling you the truth. I thought that you were
probably crying inside. Like you did when Karl
whipped you. When we're very badly hurt we prefer
to keep out tears to ourselves."

As the words sank home Michael's sight dimmed.
Black shapes surged up everywhere, from the walls,
from the bed, from his mind. The bottom of the pit: it

exists. It's within us. Why do my eyelids tremble? Why are my fists clenched? He rose, and went with uncertain steps to lean out the window. A girl passed in the street: where are you going? She was carrying a package by its string: what is in it? In the center of the square a man dusted a bench with his handkerchief and sat down: whom are you waiting for? A messenger parked his bicycle at the curb across the way, a telegram in his hand: what message do you bear?

Now or never, Michael thought. This is the moment, and it will never come again. I could justify myself very simply; explain to him that sometimes the fount of tears dries up; weeping is also a gift of heaven. I might convince him; I ought to try. If he'll only let me do it, and not put up resistance. Let me transform the image he carries congealed in his memory. But how: how do I go about it?

Michael had stood for too long at the window. When he finally turned, Yankel was no longer in the room.

He never saw the boy again until the day when a policeman summoned him urgently to the hospital.

At the beginning of December Michael went to the Prefecture of Police to have his residence permit extended. The waiting room was a buzz of indistinct sounds, as if in a factory where hope was being fabricated for some, despair for others. Seated on benches like churchgoers, the foreigners gossiped, exchanging advice in low voices and in all languages. In a glassed-in compartment at the end of the hall a mustachioed bailiff, overflowing with scorn and smugness, checked the papers before sending them on to the proper offices. His behavior demonstrated the feasibility of being in a bad mood every day of the week, during office hours. Master within this house after the President of the Republic, he missed no opportunity to remind these refugee fellows that their status was subhuman. In that enormous hall the ancient question was finally answered: "What is a human being? Someone whose papers are in order."

After hours and hours of waiting, Michael's name and number were called. The bureaucrat in charge was unsympathetic and grouchy. These people disgusted him. All alike. They couldn't have stayed where they were and just shut up, could they. Did *he* go and bother people in Hungary or Bulgaria or wherever? He studied the dossier at great length, meticulously, leafed through affidavits of all kinds, photographs, reports—but did not deign to glance at the young man seated before him. The young man was not there across from him, but within the dossier.

His studies at an end, the official launched the usual series of questions. Age, address, occupation, means of livelihood, plans for emigration, family status, why are you here, eh, why? What would become of France if the whole population of central Europe came to settle here, I ask you?

Michael answered calmly, politely, without becoming flustered, without betraying anger. Finally the precious residence permit, validated for another six months, was tossed at him like alms. Michael said thank you. The official pretended not to have heard.

Michael was in a great hurry to get out of the building. In the corridor he passed a young blonde. They halted instantly; neither could draw breath. Fire swept into their faces. And without a word they fell into each other's arms. Milika had tears in her eyes. "You, here! You here!" All she could manage was those two words. "You, here! You, here!"

"Let's get out of this place," Michael said.

Milika too had come to have her permit extended; she thought no more of it that day. She would come another time. Hers had not yet expired. She had a few days left.

They strolled along the quais, in silent communion with Szerencseváros, that blasted Paradise where all had once seemed so simple. The day was cold, but they took no notice. It was as though they were just back from a funeral, solemn and meditative, dreading the moment when they would be alone at last and have to look at each other, speak to each other, discover each other, say to each other "All right. Now what?"

"I'm tired," Milika said.

"I know. It's heavy work, carrying the dead on your back."

Milika was more beautiful, riper, more feminine. She wore a stylish fur coat. Nevertheless she was shivering. She clenched her teeth as if to hold back the flood of tears, memories, words. He asked her about Varady's death; he had not yet heard. "Yes, of course," she said, pressing his arm tighter. "But let's sit down somewhere. I'm exhausted. This leap backward has been so sudden. Let's go have a cup of coffee."

"I have no money."

She bowed her head guiltily: "I have some."

They entered a café, sat down, ordered. Milika narrated the end of the story that had fascinated three generations of Jews in Szerencseváros. The old man's suicide, his last laugh, his last wishes. It was she, Milika, who had buried him: in the garden, close by the wall.

Milika had returned to Hungary after the war, remained for some weeks, and had come to Paris at the invitation of one of Varady's old friends, a former disciple, now running a weekly newspaper in France.

One question burned at the tip of Michael's

tongue: had Varady staged that sentimental interlude under the apple tree? But he kept it to himself.

He was surprised at the void Milika filled in his heart. He had never dreamed that an unexpected meeting with her would comfort him so. The emptiness within him became a fullness. The walls seemed less formidable, less insurmountable. A woman is there, and the world is no longer the same. Suddenly everything *is*. Everything becomes simple, true, possible. I am, you are. That's enough. It means that man is not alone, that the scattered forces are somewhere reunited.

Kalman had said to him one day, "When the self of man has disappeared, crumbled away, what can remain if not love without limits, an absolutely pure love, pure of all self?" It is true that we often believe self to be gone, and are then obliged to watch it return: we believed in a mirage, the mirage of the adolescent, the mirage of the poet, the mirage of the religious and even of the intellectual. Still, there must be some true liberation in the silence of the soul—or rather in its muffled murmuring. At least this: a liberating movement of the self which has suffered enough to be transformed into love.

"Is anything wrong?" Milika asked. "You sit there so quietly, as if you were hurting."

His throat tight, he answered, "Yes, Milika. I hurt. I think of Szerencseváros and I hurt." Then in a lower tone, "Szerencseváros. The city of luck." And still lower, but direct and not dreamy: "I think I loved you. Puppy love, I know. But it was love just the same."

For an instant she only stared: her eyes grew larger, bluer, overflowed with azure, with dreams, with the past. She's going to cry, Michael thought. If she cries I'll get up and leave her.

She broke into a smile.

"What are you grinning at?"

"At you. At the little boy that survived in you."

"He didn't survive. He's dead. I deny him. Never saw him, never knew him. A stranger. An unidentified corpse. I have nothing in common with him."

"That's a shame. I was very fond of that little boy so excited about the forbidden garden. To me he stood for the future, as Varady stood for the past. In my mind you two composed a single being. I thought the little boy was immortal. But as long as I live, he lives."

Michael averted his eyes and asked, "Does he follow after you, that little boy? He follows me. I know he's dead, but I also know that he won't leave me. He follows my trail; he walks in my footsteps; I can hear his own. When I run, he runs along behind me. And you?"

"I've learned to run very fast. Faster than the dead. But the little boy isn't dead. I wouldn't like to leave him behind."

They drank their coffee and ordered again. Suddenly Milika started: it was growing late. The street lamps glowed. "That's enough talk about the past!" she cried. She asked him questions that he evaded slyly. He refused to give her his address, fearing a visit. But he took hers, and promised to call very soon. When they parted it was full night. He knew that he would never see her again.

He did not telephone. He had never intended to. The little boy is dead, the love is a dead love, Szerencseváros is a city of the dead. There is no loving in a graveyard. Love is for those who can forget, for those who seek to forget.

So he pursued his accustomed life, his wanderings, his search for a dream. He had still not found a job. To get bread, and now and then a pat of margarine, was an insoluble problem.

One night at the synagogue the man with piercing eyes presented him with a can of sardines. Having no bread, he set it aside. Two days later, still without bread, he decided to open it. He had barely bolted three sardines when he suffered a violent spasm of the stomach. He tottered to his bed and passed out.

He did not awake until the next day, when his landlady came in to clean the room. She shrieked in horror. The bed was streaked with vomit. Michael was the color of a corpse, his lips white, his forehead beaded. "What have you done, little priest?" she shouted bitterly. "Been drinking? Are you a drunkard now?"

His lips quivering, his vision fogged, Michael could only produce unintelligible sounds. Fever wracked him. There was no strength in his body. He felt empty, hollow, a membrane about to burst.

The landlady's anger rose several notches. With both hands she slapped his face, his legs; she spewed bitter complaints about the ingratitude of her tenants; invoked God and the devil; left the room and came back and left again, this time with a cup of hot tea, then with a glass of Cognac. She never ceased talking and bustling about, as if the floor were burning her feet.

Inadvertently Michael glanced at the table. The can of sardines was still there. He fell to retching again, worse than ever; he was bringing up his very guts.

The room danced before him. The landlady was transformed and became Martha, the town drunk of Szerencseváros, the witch who flung up her skirts and exposed her naked, swollen belly to drive off the children who tagged after her.

He recalled Szerencseváros, his childhood, his agonies, his tortured dreams. I'll die, he thought. I'll die in a strange land and a drunken woman with her skirts in the air will dance around my corpse. I'll die like a dog and a furious old madwoman will make love to my cold body.

Then Milika's name came to him. Milika. Her slim body, her delicate profile, the warmth that glowed in her smile. He could hear only the one word, the one name. Milika. Mi-li-ka. The name invaded his bleak room, swelled enormously, was inscribed on the ceiling, on the walls, on the landlady's menacing fingers. It was as if Milika had sent her name as a messenger exhorting him to hold out, telling him, "Don't go under; hang on; I'm here, I exist!"

"Milika," he murmured in unconscious lamentation.

"What did you say?" asked his landlady.

"Milika," he breathed again.

"Who's that? A girl friend? A relative? Say something, for God's sake! What's her address? Her phone number? I'll call her! She can come and take care of you. You can't lie here and rot all alone like that!"

Michael gritted his teeth. His chest and throat hurt, his stomach pitched. He was swimming in a sea of flame. Milika, Milika. He wanted to shout the name, to make it a prayer, an invitation. He needed all the strength still in him to keep silent; with a savage effort of will he managed to keep his lips together.

The landlady watched him struggle, and cried out in amazement: "How handsome you are like that! I've never seen you so handsome!"

"Hey! What's the trouble there? Out of your head already? What are you crying about?"

The voice brought him back to prison. He opened his eyes again: light was filtering in through the walls. Nothing had changed, but he could sense that it was daytime. The atmosphere was less dense.

"You're a disappointment to me! I thought you'd last longer."

That must have been the second officer. Michael remembered only one trip to the toilet. The officer had come in when he was already back in position, face to the wall.

"Why don't you open that ugly face of yours and tell us what we want to know?" the officer continued in a bored monotone. "*We* have time, but not you, my boy. You're going mad slowly. You're already showing the first signs. You've been whimpering and moaning aloud as if we were beating you. Pretty soon you'll start to talk and shout. You'll spill everything. We won't be able to dam the flow. You'll drain yourself."

Michael did not listen. He was examining his inner self: was he master of his body? He held his breath, released it; clenched his right fist, opened it; stuck out his tongue, withdrew it; shrugged, relaxed; tried to move his legs—and only they failed him. Too bad, he thought. Pedro is worth a pair of legs.

And now he concentrated on the functioning of his mind: are you still mine to command? Three and six are what? Who was Sakyamuni? Thales of Miletus? Xanthippe?

Having passed the examination with flying colors, Michael relaxed and let his thoughts wander freely in Szerencseváros. It is morning there. The mountains are cloaked in a delicate bluish haze. The city is like an open hand into which the sun showers its golden dust. In the main square a baker is opening his shop, the first to open today. Trees spread their branches to capture the early heat. Here and there curtains part. Churchbells toll six o'clock, or seven, or eight. Day takes the city by storm and occupies it in stages.

Michael wanders without haste, stopping at this store or that house. Here, they bought him his first wristwatch: he had just turned thirteen. There, next door, lived Itzu, a childhood friend. At the corner by the little market was Kalman's house, halfway between the prison and the insane asylum. Michael feels an urge to go and knock at the door; he holds off, afraid. Suppose Kalman came to open it?

Slowly, reluctantly, the streets are peopled. Grocers greet their early customers, all equally drawn and sleepy. Children troop to school silently in twos and threes; sleep is still upon them. Old widows in black walk to church with uneasy steps: will they be late? early? Will God be on time? The men are taciturn, the women hostile, grudging: they would rather have kept to the warmth of their homes. Among the passers-by Michael seeks a familiar face, and finds none. Then too they all look alike. They might be a single creature before a thousand distorting mirrors. Michael thinks, This is my city, I was born here. Here I became a part of time, here I was launched upon the river, here is my source, here burrow my roots: and yet here I am an unwanted stranger; just as my own memories deny me.

The people come and go, not stopping before him. They do not see him. Perhaps they are pretending. For them he is already dead. For them he has never existed. I once trod this same twisting road to the same school with the same tug at the heart, the same books under my arm. And not the slightest link now. I live in a different age.

He hears a distant laugh. He walks toward it. He turns his back to the asylum with its strangled silences, passes the cemetery with its gray-black walls, leaves Locust Street behind, and the Gypsy Road, and at the end, in front of her shack of rotting wood, Martha signals him to approach. In anguish he moves forward cautiously.

"I was waiting," she says.

Silent, Michael stares at her, squinting: finally someone is waiting for him.

"Your friends are dead," Martha says. "Dead and

gone. Your enemies won't meet your eye. Only I haven't changed. Szerencseváros is me. You were searching for me: here I am. Take me." At which she raises her skirt and twitches her naked belly obscenely.

"No!" Michael cries. "You disgust me!"

"So? All the more reason! Take me and I'll teach you absurd love, imbecile love, eternal love. Take me to take revenge, to revolt yourself. To laughter you can only oppose laughter. Show destiny that you aren't afraid of it, that it's no stranger, that you can make fun of it, laugh in its face. Shed your illusions, shed them all, let the wind scatter them; fling off a dead weight, the weight of death. Take me and carry your revolt to the end; break through to the other side of the wall."

All is silence. The river no longer flows to the sea, the trees no longer rustle, the sky is infinite. Michael looks at Martha and sees her for what she is: ugly, disgusting, rotten. An odor of dirt and excrement hovers about her body. Her hair is harsh as burnt straw. All the bones of her face are visible, projecting, threatening. Her belly is white, her skin crisscrossed with wrinkles, her thighs flabby. Michael's nostrils take in a gust of stench; he is overcome by an irrepressible desire to vomit.

"Go to it!" exhorts the old drunkard joyfully. "Vomit up a bellyful, but come to me. Be a god and act like one: be the friend of ugliness, of the inhuman. Enter within me, give me your disgust and your love. That's the only kind of love that life deserves."

Vomit in his mouth, he approaches her, hesitant, gasping, choking.

"Go to it!" she cries ecstatically. "Don't be afraid! Don't think of anything! Give me all you have, the whole accumulation! Don't hold back!"

Michael thinks, She is mad. If nothing exists but

her, there is no reason to hang back. There is no reason not to follow her into madness.

"A little while and you'll have no snap at all," the officer said in his sleepy monotone. "You'll be limp. You'll beg us to listen. You'll carry on like a drunken woman deserted by her lover. You'll want to get rid of too many things and you won't know where to begin. You'll be insane through silence. Is that what you want? All right. I don't give a damn. I like it. I like to see a man at the point where he spits out his life in words like a bitter thing he hates. But do me a favor: wait till I'm back on duty. Hold out for another twenty-four hours. I want to see the change with my own eyes. What an elevating sight! How impressive! Insanity, beginning in the legs, devouring the body bit by bit, taking possession of you gradually: thighs, back, belly, chest, neck, mouth, eyes. And then it bursts, a crystal vase smashing on stone. I like things that break, that change shape. Soon your body will lose its unity. It'll become a collection of spare parts. Your legs, your arms, your tongue, will no longer communicate one with another: each limb and organ will act for itself. Freely. They'll be free of you."

You mustn't listen to him, Michael repeated over and over. But he realized that it was becoming more and more difficult to wall himself away from the sounds of the world.

When Michael reached the hospital, out of breath, they were operating on Yankel. The corridor lay under a raw, cold light. Nurses, apparently quite busy, came and went without looking at him, as if it were normal that he be there. Now and then he asked one as she went by, "Is it very bad?" Nothing is really bad to nurses: "Everything will be all right." They learn that in training. Only the doctors are supposed to make declarations, only they are authorized to say, "It was a failure, it was a success." The others smile and reassure us: "Everything will be all right." And the worst is that we believe them.

Outside, Paris was enjoying a beautiful spring morning: the city was bursting with youth, freshness, vigor.

Michael paced the corridor like a trapped animal. The policeman had said, "Come quickly. There's been an accident." "An accident?" "Yes, Monsieur. Hurry. A truck ran over him." "Him? Who?" Michael knew. No need to ask. In his pocket, the policeman added, they had found a single name, a single address, on a sheet of notebook paper. "Come at once." It was an accident, the policeman repeated in a voice full of kindness. A stupid accident. All accidents are. The carelessness of drivers, of pedestrians, what can you expect? It happens. It could happen to anybody, couldn't it? Yes, Officer. It could happen to anybody.

The operation lasted several hours. It was past noon when the surgeon emerged. Michael leaped up and barred his path.

"Who are you?" the doctor asked. "His brother?"

Michael shook his head.

"A relative?"

"No. A friend."

"It looks bad. Very bad." The doctor avoided his eyes. Michael paled. He opened his mouth to suck in air; he was choking. He stood motionless for several moments. A nurse watched them at a distance, not daring to come closer. "The brain was damaged," the doctor went on. "The boy is lost. He's going to die."

Why does the earth gape at such moments? Why do we plunge toward the void? Michael pressed a hand to his head. An iron fist drove against his chest.

He was dropping through an ever-deeper, ever-darker pit.

"It's better that way," the doctor continued. "If the body holds out, physical or mental paralysis will follow, probably both. In his case death will be a deliverance." He was silent for an instant, and went on in a tone of annoyance, "We did all we could. You must believe me."

He turned and walked off with slow, regular steps. Michael stared after him until he had turned the corner. Soon a nurse came to tell him that Yankel was in Room 212.

His eyes ringed with dark circles, Michael went downstairs to the second floor. He felt his legs give way. How alive would the little prince be? Where did he bear the sign of death?

Still under anesthesia, Yankel was asleep. His breathing was inaudible. His unrecognizable head emerged from a mountain of dressings. A terrifying calm lay heavily on the room, a calm that seemed to radiate from the boy's body itself. The little prince, Michael thought. There he is. Vanquished, taken in the most humiliating of defeats. He departs covered with wounds. That's how he'll arrive on high, soaked in blood, in burning pain.

An immense wrath, savage and destructive, welled up suddenly in Michael. His eyes flashed. The little prince's death—this death—was too unjust, too absurd. He wanted to pit himself against the angel as Jacob had: fell him with a blow, trample him. One gesture, just one, but a gesture in proportion to his misery. He gazed about the room like a man rendered invincible by madness, seeking an object to destroy. The bed, the chair, the night table: all those were nothing. Things too small, too meaningless. The four horribly white walls: lunging, he could have reduced them to rubble. Also too easy a task. His mind inflamed, he started in all directions, rushing. Abruptly he halted, stiffened. Obeying an imperious command, he fell to his knees and brought his face close to the boy's. "Little prince," he murmured, "little prince, you're slipping away, and taking the memory of me with you, the memory of someone who didn't cry when his father met death. I hated you, I loved you; I hated you because I hated myself, and I loved you for the same reason. Do you hear me?" Michael stretched out trembling hands to caress him. He raised the blanket gently and saw the neck, delicate and slim. "Can you hear me, little prince? I'm talking to the memory of myself imprisoned in your mind. It's easy to shed tears; much harder, so much harder, to go on living without having wept." Michael stared at the boy's throat and trembled. Unknowingly he set his hands upon it. At first with infinite tenderness. Then a shuddering swept him from head to foot, a tremor that was born in the depths of time. He did not understand what was happening to him, but yielded to the blinding strength that flowed from his body. It broke through, shattered the dikes. Involuntarily he squeezed the neck harder, harder, in a raging fury. Yankel's face turned blue. Michael's teeth chattered like a lunatic's, but he went on squeezing, determined to strangle his own despair.

Luckily the door opened. Jolted out of a nightmare, Michael relaxed his embrace. He raised his fingers before his swollen, unsated eyes; he wanted to bite into them.

"He's asleep," the doctor said. "Let him sleep. He'll pass away in his sleep. It's better that way. He won't suffer."

Michael sat up with great difficulty to face the doctor. His fingers weighed him down; they were clutching at the void. He tried to hide them behind his back, but they refused to take direction. Ashamed,

Michael looked at the doctor and shook his head, his useless head, from side to side. How big he was, the doctor, how well set-up, healthy, terribly healthy. He filled the room.

"Don't be ashamed," the doctor said. "Have yourself a cry; it's a relief."

"I'd rather not be relieved."

Together they stared at the tiny face, already shadowed by the beating of the wings of death. The doctor sighed: "But you've got to express what you feel. Otherwise a man would burst. How to express it is the problem."

"I know how," Michael said. They were talking, but their eyes never left Yankel: they were speaking to him.

"You know?"

"Yes, I know." And without changing expression Michael gave way to a powerful, manly laugh, a blood-chilling laugh. Shocked, the doctor stared at him; the doctor slumped, and tears came. "I prefer my method," he said. He attempted a vague gesture of friendship toward Michael, wanting to take his hand, or squeeze his shoulder. But that laugh, like a rigid mask for loneliness, stood between them, condemning them separately. The doctor slumped wearily, wiped his eyes, and went out.

Michael knelt near the bed again. In a short while Yankel opened his eyes. Michael held his breath: was he coming back to life? "Look at me, Yankel! It's me, your friend! I'm here, little prince. Look at me. Keep your eyes on me. Don't look away!"

The boy stared out blindly, immobile, not even blinking. Michael felt suddenly that someone was standing behind him. He turned abruptly: no one. And yet he felt a presence in the room, even an odor, an awareness. Only then did he understand that death is something other, something more, than the simple absence of life. Life may quit a body, a consciousness, but death does not necessarily follow. Just as death may invade a creature though life has not yet departed.

Yankel's agony lasted seven days and seven nights. Michael never left his bedside. He would see death's talons, hear the beat of its wings, hear it snicker. Sometimes the anguish was so violent that he cried out, "Leave the boy alone! Take me! Don't be so sly; you want a battle; I'm ready; but leave the boy alone!" His cries found no echo. Then he went to the window, opened it wide, as if to invite the wind into his being and the night into his soul. He leaned out. His glance swept the deserted street. He breathed deeply to convince himself that he was still alive, and broke into laughter again, with a passion beyond all despair.

The doctor stopped by several times a day. He examined the boy's dilated pupils and murmured, "Perhaps tonight." And Michael, gaunt and hollow-cheeked, echoed him: "Yes, perhaps tonight." And within himself he said, The little prince is hanging on, he doesn't want to go.

Every hour a nurse came in and jolted him out of his torpor: "Time for an injection." Michael wanted to ask, "Why bother, if we're waiting so impatiently for death?" But he said nothing. He watched her as she worked; followed intently the agile fingers preparing the syringe and then driving the needle into the pink and white skin. He no longer turned away. Earlier he had not been able to stand the sight of Yankel's injections; he trembled and closed his eyes. Not now. On the contrary, now he insisted on seeing everything, resolved as he was that nothing of his friend's slow death would remain alien to him.

Michael remembered the legends of the Talmud

about wise men who stopped children in the street to cull truth from their lips. If Yankel could talk now, he thought, he would unveil the mysteries. It is he who would tell me if life is only a spasm of nothingness. But Yankel did not speak. He lay open-mouthed and wide-eyed, but no word, no message, emerged.

Michael no longer noticed externals. He did not hear the nurses come and go. Now and then he caught a glimpse of the doctor, whose voice grew lower and softer, repeating the same phrase always: "Let's hope it's tonight."

"I was on the verge of madness," I said.

Pedro listened intently, his head bowed slightly. He was smoking his pipe, and occasionally his face was like a portrait on a canvas of white smoke.

"I talked to Yankel and he couldn't hear me," I went on. "I spoke to his eyes, to the death they harbored. I consumed myself. I refused to eat, to sleep, to run away. I was trying to justify my existence, and also to understand the need for that justification, a need that pressed down on me like a suffocating dream. Out of the little prince's death I was creating an absolute value. It became a prism through which I judged acts and beings. Everything revolved around it. It seemed to me that my only purpose in life was to be present at the death agonies of a future that was, at bottom, mine too. I wove a universe of hallucinations. I blended the past with the future. All the men on earth bore a single face: that of my dying friend. Their destinies were measured by his. A child who dies becomes the center of the universe: stars and meadows die with him."

Pedro stared deeply into my eyes as if the truth lay buried behind them. I was hoping he wouldn't cry. I preferred him strong, proud, truculent.

"I was on the verge of madness," I said again. "It was there, at the end of the road I'd taken. I could snuggle up to it as if it were a cloak to keep me warm. I could touch it. More than that: I could see myself in it. I saw myself as I was and as I wanted to be. I was at once myself and another. I'd finally been freed from myself."

Pedro made no movement, but I had to stop for breath. In reliving the encounter with madness I had begun to tremble again, body and soul. Once more I was climbing a high mountain, and when I reached the peak I had to concentrate desperately to resist the temptation to jump. The man who chooses death is following an impulse of liberation from the self; so is the man who chooses madness. A last resort, it awaits us open-armed. Like a pool down in the valley it beckons us: "Come! Never fear! Jump! Banish fear forever!" To keep our balance then is the most difficult and absurd struggle in human existence.

"After seven days and seven nights," I went on, "his suffering finally ended. Time congealed in his wide, staring eyes. Panicky shadows pressed together, merging finally in one opaque mass. My heartbeats thudded like cannon shots; misery consumed me. The earth had tilted on its axis, and the sun had ceased to govern it. It was at that moment that I was most tempted to take the leap, to become another. Just to say yes, to acquiesce with a nod, would have been enough; to roll on the floor, stick out my tongue, break into song, howl like a hurt dog: safety was there within reach, and detachment, deliverance.

"I resisted. I said no."

"You go beyond the Nazarene," Pedro mocked me. "Let your no mean no; but let your yes mean no too. You want to do better, surpass him, exceed. You have the soul of a priest: your landlady was right. Christ *said no only to men; you say no to God. You're jealous of God."*

"Possible, Pedro, possible. But in this case I might have reached the kingdom of madness simply by saying yes: no more torment, no more problems, no more anguish. Since the beginning of history madmen have represented the divine presence: the light in their eyes comes bathed in the source. But I can't have that too comfortable, too easy escape. The choice of madness is an act of courage. It can't be done more than once. It's an end in itself. An act of the free will that destroys freedom. Freedom is given only to man. God is not free."

Pedro broke into applause, laughing: "I like you, my friend! You're trying to drive God mad. That's why I like you."

I thought: And God too is trying to drive me mad.

The doctor dropped a hand to his shoulder: "It's all over."

Michael stood up, his legs unsteady. His glance refused to quit that livid, immobile corpse which an hour before had been the guarantee of his own survival. He thought, That's Yankel. And immediately a question: Is it still he? That body without life, without future, without change? Tomorrow it will be rotten and the earth will have absorbed it; the final loss of identity. The little prince, a handful of dust?

Michael allowed himself to be led away. At the door he turned for a last look. A last look before leaving him, before deserting him.

They walked side by side down the corridor, which seemed longer and emptier than usual. Michael did not know where the doctor was taking him. He had no wish to know. He wondered if it was day or night.

"Did you laugh?" asked the doctor quietly.

"No, Doctor. I didn't laugh."

"Did you cry?"

"No, Doctor. I didn't cry." And after a moment: "He cried, Doctor. It was the second time I saw him cry."

The memory possessed his mind while his legs bore him mechanically along with the doctor. A few minutes before dying, the little prince had wept silently. Transparent tears had flowed and flowed. His open eyes had seemed two inexhaustible springs. When he had already passed from life, the tears were trickling down his inert face. They had survived him.

The doctor ushered Michael into his office, indicated a leather armchair, a couch, cigarettes. "I could stay with you," he suggested timidly. "I could listen to you." He hesitated, and corrected himself: "I'd *like* to listen to you."

The room was hazy in a shadowy twilight. Was it day or night? Both. Michael slumped into the armchair and closed his eyes. Without a word the doctor left, closing the door softly behind him. Michael heard him from far off and thought, That is how little princes leave this world: delicately, with no noise. He clutched his head and prayed, "Oh, God! Make me be silence! Make me be! Be . . ."

"What is the death of a child?" Pedro asked.

"An injustice," I answered.

"No. That would be making a moral problem out of it. It's more. It's a question mark. Before, what were you? Something potentially alive. Since then, worse luck, you've lived!" He pulled at his pipe, blew out a cloud of white smoke, and added, "Because life's like that. It's when you are alive that you have to say 'Worse luck!'" His deep, melancholy voice was so dynamic, so alive, that nothing else existed. Pedro was no longer a body, but a voice. His whole being reposed in his voice. I thought: If it falls silent his life is ended. If it falls silent my own life will end.

"It's the divine will," he went on, "that if a man has something to say, he says it most perfectly by taking unto him a woman and creating a new man. And then God remembers that he too has something to say; and he entrusts the message to the Angel of Death. But even so, your creation isn't a total loss. Something of it persists. A question, and that's a lot. Suddenly you become aware of the agony of living, of seeing loneliness, of seeing pain, of seeing agony. The dialogue—or the duel, if you like—between man and his God doesn't end in nothingness. Man may not have the last word, but he has the last cry. That moment marks the birth of art."

"And of friendship," I said.

"Friendship is an art."

I said nothing. Pedro smoked and tilted his head, as if to hear his own heart. Then he said, "I don't know if the sky has darkened or if the night is within me while I speak to you. But like a dream, the most real dream, the only real one, my voice comes, saying that there are only two possibilities for me: either I suffer your pain with you, or I'll suffer it without you; in a common absence, I mean. In any case I'll suffer it."

If his voice falls silent his life will end, I repeated. For me it's different. It's when I'm silent that I live; in silence I define myself.

Pedro stopped smiling suddenly and I was afraid. His face grew hard: "You're my friend and I want to know everything."

I trembled, my breathing quickened, my nostrils flared. He wants to know everything, I thought. He isn't afraid to know everything.

"Did you want the little prince to die? Answer me!"

"Please, Pedro, please. Don't ask me any questions!"

"Is that why you want to go backwards in time? To become a child—and die?"

"Don't ask me questions, Pedro!"

Pedro transfixed me with a long look, until a burst of shouting carried him away.

The officer was hammering the table with his fist. He was shouting. He was furious: "Talk, for the love of God! Open up! Stop playing games! Why did you come back? Who helped you?"

Michael listened as though the man were speaking to someone else. He's not talking to me; it's not I who stand here, a mute spectator. It's not Michael. Michael is gone. gone with the little prince.

A sharp, burning pain shot through him, striking now at his ears, now at his eyes, his back, his arms. The officer shouted louder. His voice penetrated the prisoner's mind in a deafening buzz and ravaged it. Michael thought of the yogis who can substitute a pure void for their consciousness. For them physical immobility induces immobility of the spirit. Not for Michael. On the contrary: the longer his body stands rigid, the stronger and more vigorous his thoughts, the faster they proliferate. Upright, facing the wall, he finds himself able to hear a thousand voices at a time, each distinct, to see a thousand paths, to weigh a thousand destinies. He listens to the officer, but that isn't the only voice yammering at him. There are others: Varady, Milika, Kalman, Yankel. His sensibilities sharpen, his being opens: as to the Rabbi of Nicholsburg, all the sounds and echoes of land and sea come to him. He senses even the ultra-sounds that certain creatures, and certain destinies, give off. He understands now why man is drawn toward martyrdom, why he inflicts upon himself barely imaginable suffering: his life is not enough, he wants the life of others to beat in his veins, he wants to annex the cries and tears of the blemished and ruined who fight and despair.

"Why?" shouted the officer.

"Why?" asked a blonde girl, sad and vibrant. Why did you run from me? A boy glances up at him feverishly, questioningly: why did they throw me into the black hole? And Kalman, murmuring into his yellowed beard: why have you not said your prayer today? And Hersh-Leib: why aren't your legs made of wood?

Outside it is midday. At its zenith the sun follows its subjects, who play at being men here below. The butcher wipes his forehead on an apron blotched with blood. The grocer says to his wife, "Go and eat. I'll be along later." The clockmaker, behind his window, watches the passers-by: today again he will go without lunch. Since his wife's death he takes no pleasure in meals. For the lonely, eating becomes a torture. He inspects the passersby; badly adjusted timepieces, marking different hours.

Finally the spokesman for all the "whys" fell silent. A great silence spread through the temple. The door opened. Two guards came to take the prisoner to the toilet.

Michael walked cautiously and with great difficulty; an immense weight crushed down on his shoulders. I have no more legs, he thought; I have only two crutches.

His teeth chattered.

Third Prayer

MICHAEL TELEPHONED PEDRO ON THE DAY HE WAS scheduled to leave Tangier. Meir, his smuggler friend in Paris, had said, "My liaison in Tangier is an odd sort of fellow. You'd find him interesting." Michael took his telephone number out of politeness; he had not the slightest desire to enter circles in which nothing was talked about but money, exchange rates, borders, black markets.

"May I speak to Pedro?"

"Who is this?" asked a voice full of authority.

"A friend of Meir."

"Michael?"

"Yes."

"I've been waiting three weeks for your call. Meir told me to take care of you. Why the delay?"

Michael mumbled excuses: too busy, he had a dozen pieces to write, time was short; he had only finished his assignment late the previous night.

"All right. Come to see me tonight."

"I won't be able to. I'm taking the train out late this afternoon. I have to get on to Casablanca. Friends are waiting for me. We came down here together."

109

"You can leave tomorrow."

Michael tried to raise objections, but Pedro cut him off curtly. "At eleven tonight I'll be waiting at the Black Cat. It's in the Soco Chico. Be there." He hung up.

Michael's hesitations were only momentary. Something in Pedro's voice roused his curiosity. Voices interested him more than acts. He pictured Meir's friend as a cruel, unapproachable gangster of sinister aspect. He decided to stay over until the next day, and not to reject any encounter.

A week later he was still in Tangier.

It was to Meir that he owed his trip to North Africa. Meir had run into him in the street and gasped in horror: Michael was like a man half mad. Unshaved, hunched, his eyes haggard, his manner unheeding, there was something of the beggar in him, something of the sleepwalker, something of the *poète maudit*. He was talking to himself, laughing all alone.

"Michael!" cried Meir, blocking his path.

Michael studied him for a long moment, apparently not recognizing him. Then he broke into tears and laughter simultaneously.

"What's the matter?" Meir asked uneasily.

"I'm sick. Very sick. Sick of living, sick of walking, sick of laughing."

Meir hailed a taxi and took Michael to his own hotel. He sent for a doctor, whose diagnosis was simple, "Overstrain," and who administered an injection. Michael sank into a deep sleep, and only awoke twenty-four hours later.

Seated at his bedside, Meir smiled: "You really scared me, you know."

"I thought you were immune to fear," Michael said. He was exhausted. He had not returned to his room since Yankel's death. He had wandered the streets aimlessly, sleeping on a bench, beneath a bridge, sharing the life, and the meals, of the bums. Occasionally when he was at the very end of his rope he spent the night in a mission shelter, where they gave him a little soup, bread, and black coffee in return for a prayer to the Lord. But he resorted to that only when he could no longer endure the hunger and fatigue that were destroying him.

"How could it come to this?" Meir asked. "Tell me."

"There's nothing to tell. Anybody can get sick." He had learned to keep his pain to himself; when all else was lost pain kept him company, gave him an identity.

Meir did not press the point. He kept Michael with him for several weeks, until the young man was back on his feet. Then he suggested a trip: "Get out of Europe. It'll do you good. Next week three of my men are going to Casa by way of Spain, Tangier, and Spanish Morocco. You ought to join them."

"What for? To be a smuggler? You forget, I'm not particularly gifted that way."

"I haven't forgotten, don't worry. For smuggling I have people somewhat less lacking in talent."

"Then what would I do?"

"Nothing. Rest. Learn how to live again. Enjoy life."

Michael declined the offer. He had no desire to live as a sponger off his friend. But Meir refused to let it rest. The next day he announced. "I have good news for you. I've got some connections in the newspaper business, you know. You're a reporter now. A Paris weekly has agreed to publish your travel diary. The pay is good. What do you say?"

"Who do you know on a weekly?"

"The publisher's wife, or his mistress, I'm not sure which. A girl from home. You probably remember her. Milika."

Michael's heart stopped. Milika. Shocked, he turned pale. Meir noticed nothing.

"I talked to her about you. She fixed it up with her husband, unless he's her lover. Do you want to meet her?"

After a pause Michael said, "No." Milika, he thought. Milika married. Milika mistress. Milika here, alive.

"What about it?" Meir was impatient. "Will you go?"

"Yes."

"In Tangier I have a contact named Pedro. An odd sort of fellow. You'll find him interesting."

"No doubt," Michael said.

Late in the afternoon Michael left the Hotel El-Mabrouk. His appointment was some hours away. He had time, and decided to devote it to a last stroll through the city. He liked walking alone in the narrow, gloomy alleyways of the swarming agglomeration—Gibraltar's eternal open window on Africa.

Tangier was washed in a velvety bluish twilight. Moneychangers' booths stood like a row of ghosts at the entrance to the Soco Chico. A melancholy quiet had replaced the polyglot sounds of the day.

In the marketplace the old storyteller was reciting the same tale he recited every night, rousing as much enthusiasm in his audience as if it were the first time. Squatting around the ascetic old man some hundred Arabs punctuated the story at appropriate moments by laughter, exclamations of joy, cries of horror. Michael thought that if he were to live another life he would want to be a teller of tales: since the first man and to the end of time, the human voice remains the one instrument by which men can share their dreams and secrets.

Night was falling darker; the old man's unvarying

voice seemed to come from far off. Near Michael an Arab sat sleeping; even in his sleep he contributed *Ohs* and *Ahs* and assorted gabbles whenever the recital demanded the participation of a chorus. Michael thought, There sits a happy man. Awake or asleep, the same uninterrupted dream spanned his days and nights.

He leaned forward slightly to contemplate the sleeper: so comfortable, so peaceful, nodding. Michael's thoughts spoke to him: you are happy, servant of Allah. You're probably illiterate; you've never heard of nuclear fission or Heinrich von Kleist. The problem of the immortality of the soul leaves you indifferent; knowing whether Hegel was profoundly religious or profoundly atheistic does not trouble your mind. You're happy. Allah is great, and if what he accomplishes is not, that's his affair and not yours. You just sleep. One day is like another, one dream is like another, men repeat the same stories always, the rivers flow to the sea: why torture yourself? Why covet what your life lacks? Why run off to distant places if Allah is great everywhere, in sleep as in happiness, in joy as in forgetfulness? Right, you are right, sleep. Peace be with you, faithful servant of Allah. Tomorrow you will welcome a new day no different from yesterday. You'll marvel at the timeless bravura of the snake charmer, you'll come back to smoke your hookah, you'll stare into empty space, and night will find you here again: nothing will have changed. Happy those who close their eyes: for them nothing changes.

The Arab raised his head suddenly and noticed him. For a brief instant the man hesitated between surprise and fright: what did that foreigner want of him? What was he doing, staring at him, staring so closely? But that passed in a flash. He fell asleep again; the foreigner had merely entered the wrong dream.

The storyteller fell to his knees; his voice grew staccato. His forehead and beard running with sweat, he gesticulated, struggled against the invisible forces, or the forces visible only to him, without which any story would be empty. In his hypnotized audience tension grew by the minute. The crowd held its breath as one man.

Michael guessed that the tale was approaching its end. The happy ending—the merciful intervention of Allah, the miracle—was near. The Arabs waited avidly, openmouthed, to greet it with a thunderous uproar. All's well that ends well. On high someone is watching, someone is smiling.

Dreading that effusion of mass exuberance, Michael rose and walked away hastily.

At eleven sharp, beneath the sign of a fat black cat licking its paws lazily, he silently pushed open the door of the café. He stopped on the sill: a mass of smoke urged him back. At the far end of the room—it looked like a tavern—he saw, through the smoky light, the only table that showed signs of life. Under the amused eyes of a tall bravo with hard features, a few men were getting drunk as they smoked.

Uneasy, Michael stood still for a moment. The smoke bit into his eyes, burned his chest. His heart pounded as if he faced an unexpected danger.

The celebrants, a dozen or so, were deviling an effeminate young Muslin named Yussuf. "Hey, Yussuf, where's your beautiful wife?" Yussuf rubbed his chin, laughed, and answered, "Out cheating on me, the slut!" The others egged him on: "With who, Yussuf? With who?" The young Muslim laughed louder. "With who? With my revered father, naturally! Who else would she cheat on me with?" "Bravo, bravo!" shouted the others. "He stole my wife from me, and she stole my father from me!" The others found that funny:

"Right, Yussuf. The world's full of thieves. That's the way things are. Nothing you can do about it!" Yussuf grimaced ferociously: "Some day I'll take my dagger. . . ." His audience stirred excitedly: "Then what, Yussuf? Go on!" Yussuf clenched his fist: "Some day I'll take my dagger, and slice the two of them in bits, and throw them to the jackals!" His friends were not satisfied; they clamored for the end of the story: "Why wait? Why not do it now?" Yussuf passed a hand over his lips: "No. Not yet. I like to hate. It's the breath of my life. I'll keep it in me a while longer." He fell silent suddenly, a strange gleam in his eyes. Michael looked at the tall man: a block of silent marble.

Then it was Yussuf's turn to attack. He turned to the man at his right, a wavy-haired Spaniard with tears in his eyes who seemed to be hearing a distant lamentation. "Hey, Luis!" he shouted. "Where do you keep your hate?" Luis smiled sadly. "I lost it, amigo. I don't know where it is now." "Then look for it! Hey? What do you say?" The Spaniard shook his head, woebegone: "Too late. I have no idea where it is. Probably taking a trip around the world." He began a story of the civil war: "I fought for Franco. I lived through the seige of the Alcazar. Wounded. Left on the battlefield, lying in my own blood. The Reds charging me as though I were the fortress they wanted to storm. I'm going to die." He knew both sides got rid of the wounded as soon as possible. "No more than a minute to live." He closed his eyes, mumbled a prayer. "Suddenly, a voice. I opened my eyes. A face. Twisted with rage. A German Communist, a doctor. Bullets raining around us. Son-of-a-bitching Fascist vermin, filthy murdering bastard! As he cursed, the doctor treated him: stopped the bleeding, made a dressing. Then he looked me straight in the eye, and with no warning he spat in my face." On that day Luis had lost his taste for battle, said good-bye to war, to organized cruelty. "That spit washed away my hate. Everybody today ought to learn to spit." Luis's voice cracked. He stroked his face with nervous fingers, seeking an invisible scar. His audience blustered vaguely and emptied their glasses. Michael looked at the tall man: he was saying nothing.

Luis's foggy glance wandered around the table and halted at a giant of a man continually scratching at his wild, bushy beard. "Vassili," Luis said timidly, "you call yourself a Romanian and a sculptor. Is it true, what they say? That you're not either?" Vassili boomed out a laugh that shook the walls. "My poor amigo, that's not what you should have asked me!" Luis bowed his head in shame. Vassili took pity on him: "It doesn't matter. But you have to know how to ask questions. Trouble with you Spaniards is, you're only interested in answers. Ask me to tell you about fear." Luis hastened to comply: "Tell us about fear." The giant laughed again and said, "If you insist, I will. I'll tell you all about it. It was during the last war. . . ." A spy story, agents parachuted into occupied France. Vassili was captured. The Gestapo forced two bottles of Cognac down his throat. "But I didn't talk. Fear kept me company, in a state of permanent alert." Even within his drunkenness fear was like an island of lucidity. He took refuge in it. "Ah, my friends! Blessed be the Lord who has given us fear! Thanks to fear I am multiplied, I speak in the plural like kings! I'd give everything for one moment of fear. Everything!"

Michael listened, his chest tight. The scene was unreal; am I dreaming? he wondered.

Vassili tugged at his beard as if he wanted to hurt himself. Luis had still not raised his head. Yussuf was rubbing his chin. The drinkers filled their glasses and began teasing their sculptor friend, mouthing "Brrrrr" as if they were shivering in fear. But suddenly the laughter stopped. The tall man, who had not until then opened his mouth, began to speak.

"Listen, my friends. The effects of fear are many and varied. It paralyzes some and makes others stronger. Nietzsche writes somewhere, 'What doesn't destroy me makes me stronger.' Those whom fear doesn't break it strengthens. That only happens among men gifted with flayed sensibilities, with inflamed imaginations: artists, ascetics. In attacking fear they mold their works of art, their visions of God."

Who is he? Michael wondered, holding his breath. A philosopher of the lower depths? A poet who has chosen exile? Sakyamuni among the evildoers? He spoke a melodious French, his accent a touch lordly. His voice was emotional, vibrant; it traced a furrow of shadow in the shadows. It suggested endless meadows, gloomy forests, immense solitudes. To some it brought disquiet, to others, peace. It was the dagger that opened the wound and the balm that healed it.

The others, hanging on his words, nodded in agreement. What force rivets him to them? Michael wondered, trembling. For those men, each so different from the others, Nietzsche might mean an underworld boss and art a good tip on the black market. They accepted what the tall man told them without understanding a word of it. They admired him, feared him; he possessed a power over them. They addressed themselves to him, spoke up only because he was there to hear them; they let themselves go only to enrich him inwardly. They offered him their impulses so that he might rescue them from the mud and purify them. They take him for God, Michael thought. That's why he's so alone; why he sees so far.

Michael took a step forward.

This time they heard him. They all turned to him, expressionless, hostile. He had interrupted their game, overheard their secrets. No one said a word. Time ceased to flow. The air thickened, grew heavier.

"You're Michael," said the tall man. He stared interminably at Michael. Until then Michael had not realized that his glance was so sharp: it cut like a sword. Michael had to call on all his pride to keep from flinching.

"You're Michael," the other said again.

"Yes."

"Come on over and take a chair."

With firm steps Michael walked over to sit between Luis and an Arab. Vassili pushed a glass toward him and filled it with vodka, but Michael did not touch it. He thought, I wanted to be free and strong, and I am. The power of that man, so tall and so somber, is the power to awaken me to freedom.

"Drink," the tall man said to him. "Drink up, and tell us a story."

"Ah, yes, yes!" the others chimed in. "Tell us a story. . . ."

Exhilaration swept them again: children tired of being good. They applauded, winked, licked their lips, and demanded a story.

"I'll tell you a story," Michael said. "I'll drink later." He picked up a cigarette loose on the table. He remembered what Kalman had told him one day: sometimes it happens that we travel for a long time without knowing that we have made the long journey solely to pronounce a certain word, a certain phrase, in a certain place. The meeting of the place and the word is a rare accomplishment, on the scale of humanity.

He burrowed in his memory, and searched carefully. He turned pages, weighed episodes, examined the faces buried pell-mell in his depths. Finally he knew, from the trembling of his heart, that he had found what he wanted.

The cigarette between his lips, he lit a match. It wavered in his hand. He was mildly ashamed of that. If he had never told the story of little Mendele, it was precisely because he had been afraid he would be unable to control his emotions. Little Mendele's death deserved more, more than this trembling of the fingers.

"The hero of my story," Michael began, "is neither fear nor hatred; it is silence. The silence of a five-year-old Jew. His name was Mendele. In his eyes the whole sweep of his people's sufferings could be read. He lived in Szerencseváros, which means in Hungarian the city of luck. One day the Germans decided to rid the country of what they called the Jewish plague. Feige, Mendele's mother, a beautiful and pious young widow, had a visit then from an old friend of her husband, a peasant who owned an isolated farm on the other side of the mountain.

" 'Take your son, Feige, and come with me,' the peasant said to her. 'I owe it to my friend to save his family. Hurry up, now!'

"It was night. The streets were deserted. The peasant led the widow and her son to where he had left his wagon. He had them get up into it, and then he said to them: 'I'm going to load the wagon. You'll be buried under a mountain of hay. It has to be done. I'll work out two openings so you can breathe. But be careful! In heaven's name, be careful! Don't move! Whatever happens, don't budge! And most of all when we leave town, at the sentry station! Tell that to your son, Feige.'

"The widow took her son's face in her hands and as she stroked his hair very gently she said to him, 'Did you hear? We must be silent. Whatever happens! It's our only chance. Our lives depend on it. Even if you're afraid, even if you hurt, don't call out, and don't cry! You can scream later, you can cry later. Do you understand, Son?'

" 'Yes, Mother, I understand. Don't worry. I won't cry. I promise.'

"At the sentry station two Hungarian gendarmes, black feathers in their hats, asked the peasant where he was going.

" 'I'm going home,' he answered. 'I have two farms, two fields; the town lies between them. To move hay or wheat from one to the other I've got to cross the city. I've done it so often that the horses know the way all by themselves.'

" 'What are you hiding underneath?'

" 'Nothing, officers. Nothing at all. I swear it. I have nothing to hide.'

"The gendarmes drew their long swords from their black scabbards and drove them into the hay from all angles. It went on forever. Finally the peasant couldn't stand it any longer; he let out a whimper, and tried to smother it with the back of his hand. Too late. One of the gendarmes had noticed. The peasant had to unload the hay; and the gendarmes, triumphant, saw the widow and her son.

" 'Mama,' Mendele wept, 'it wasn't me who called out! It wasn't me!'

"The gendarmes ordered him off the wagon, but he couldn't move. His body was run through. 'Mama,' he said again, while bloody tears ran into his mouth, 'it wasn't me, it wasn't me!' The widow, a crown of hay about her head, did not answer. Dead. She too had kept silence."

When Michael finished, a thick silence fell. Michael thought, I didn't tremble, I spoke in an even tone right to the end; I was calm, cold, impassive.

Yussuf, forgetting to stroke his chin, sat with his mouth open. Luis was crying. Vassili held an empty glass; he might have shattered it by the strength of his grip.

A fist crashed down on the table; bottles and glasses danced. "Drink up!" cried the tall man. "Drink up, quick!" There was so much despair in his voice that Michael looked up at him. Their eyes met with such intensity that sparks seemed to jump the gap.

"Come on, drink!"

They filled their glasses and drained them angrily. The law of strong men, pitilessly proud; they drown evil in drink or blood, but not in words.

Soon afterward the party broke up. The drinkers said good-bye to Michael by shaking his hand, touching his elbow, or patting his shoulder. The tall man and he were left face to face.

"When we think we've had it, when things get too rotten, we gather here. We drink; and instead of shrinking our memories we enlarge them, we make room for legends, and lives not our own. But you? What do you do when you've had enough, when the load is too heavy?"

"I laugh," Michael said.

The other stared intently at him. "Some day you must teach me to laugh."

"Someday I'll teach you, Pedro."

Michael was about to ask him a very simple question, so simple that ordinarily men waste it, asking it without meaning: "Who are you?" He passed it over in silence. Pedro would have answered, "I am. Isn't that enough?"

"Let's go out," Pedro suggested.

They let the night swallow them up. A pale moon reigned shyly among silvery stars. Michael breathed fresh air deep within his lungs. The city was serene. In the distance the sea played with the sky. The Soco Chico was asleep, all its windows dark. At the corner of an alleyway an Arab snored. Michael thought of the road he had traveled. He had never suspected that at its end a friend would be waiting.

"You like to walk?" Pedro asked.

"Very much."

"Let's walk."

For an hour they talked about simple day-to-day things. Michael told him about the reporter's job. He spoke with enthusiasm, even with passion: you feel humanity throbbing, you find yourself at the nerve center of history, you explore the secrets of the gods. In turn Pedro, smiling, advertised the charms of the adventurer's life.

When they ended up in front of the Hotel El-Mabrouk Pedro asked him if he had to leave in the morning. Michael said yes; they were waiting for him in Casa.

"Don't leave. Not yet."

"I must, Pedro."

"Too bad."

It would soon be dawn. Tongues of flame rose from the earth, setting the horizon aglow. Michael realized suddenly that he had reached a turning point: he was living through one of those moments when destiny sat up and took notice. He felt his heart leap. He was at a crossroads. Left or right? Whatever his choice, it would determine the future.

Pedro looked up to watch the sky change color. Who is he, really? Michael wondered uneasily. Could I spend the rest of my life puzzling over that riddle? What do I know about him? I know that he's something out of legend, who must live only at night to keep from vanishing away. I know that he is whole, cut from a solid block, inflexible, not afraid to confront death with his acts. I know all that, yet the knowledge may not reflect him, but only me. Pedro is one of those men who cannot be defined in words. Words are too small to imprison him.

"Look at the sky," Pedro said. "It's getting light. The night's disappearing."

Michael looked up. Night was disappearing, dragging behind it dark gray clouds fringed with red. The renewed mystery of the creation, Michael thought. After creating the universe, says the cabala, God smashed his tools. Why? To avoid repeating himself?

"Look at the sky," Pedro said. "If you weren't careful it could make off with some part of you and offer it up to the night in appeasement."

"The night wouldn't settle for so little."

"You don't know the night."

"Yes I do, Pedro. I know it."

Pedro went taut. He gazed directly into Michael's eyes. "Tell me," he said.

"No. Not now. Not yet. My strength isn't concentrated yet. I want to blaspheme, and I can't quite manage it. I go up against Him, I shake my fist, I froth with rage, but it's still a way of telling Him that He's there, that He exists, that He's never the same twice, that denial itself is an offering to His grandeur. The shout becomes a prayer in spite of me. On the day when the shout remains pure, I'll tell you about it."

"You're wrong," Pedro said. "The way is no less important than the goal. He who thinks about God, forgetting man, runs the risk of mistaking his goal: God may be your next-door neighbor."

They were quiet. Pedro set a hand on the young man's shoulder as if to protect him. Michael felt an impulse to ask him, "Tell me the truth, Pedro: are *you* God?" He shivered suddenly.

"Pedro," he was astonished to hear himself say, "I'm not going." At which he turned away from his friend, who did not seem at all surprised.

Michael stayed in Tangier for a whole week. He

saw Pedro every evening, either with the crowd or alone. Both men liked nocturnal wanderings, and neither got to bed before dawn.

Sometimes they walked in silence side by side. Michael discovered the texture of silence, its depths, its music. They walked, and the steps echoing more or less together off the sidewalk said: No, you are not alone, but two, two, two. Michael realized that silence was not an emptiness but a presence. The presence of God when one is alone against the world. God: I feel my own breath and know that it is not lost, that something hears it; I feel that I am at the core of something, which is perhaps Time, whose existence is proved by the beating of my heart. Or the presence of Mendele when we are alone with someone who moves us, with someone who leans toward us. Perhaps I am dead; perhaps you, too. Mendele, no. Do you hear our steps in the silence, friend? The steps are us; the silence is Mendele. It is the silence that sets off our steps.

Pedro talked about his friends. He reported that Vassili was married and Luis a bachelor, while poor Yussuf, since his domestic misadventure, was leaning toward homosexuality. The way in which Vassili, the Romanian giant, had been snatched up by a woman he did not know deserved to be mentioned. He had gone to visit friends one evening. Ten or a dozen people were there. Someone asked him why he was still a bachelor. He answered, "Before, women wanted me and I wasn't interested; today, who'd still want me?" At which a total stranger with flaming hair stood up and shot a single word at him, defiantly: "Me." Three weeks later they were married.

"I believe in simplicity," Pedro said. "When one loves, one must say: I love you. When one wants to weep, one must say: I want to weep. When one becomes aware that existence is too heavy a burden, one must say: I want to die. There will always be someone to lend an ear."

They were pacing the filthy alleyways of the Soco Chico. The walls exhaled an odor of sweat; the night was heavy, thick. "Always," Michael thought. Whenever I use that word I feel like a liar. In your mouth it rings true. Nothing of you is false. And you call yourself a smuggler! He wanted to ask, "Just what does it mean to be a smuggler?" Pedro would have answered, "Who says it means anything?" Pedro evades questions about his identity.

"In driving Adam out of Paradise," Pedro went on, "God merely deprived him of the power of simplicity. Suddenly an apple was not just an apple; the serpent was a symbol, something other than a serpent; God himself was something other than an appeal to the infinite, a need to exist, a thirst for the absolute. To look at men you'd say that all they wanted was to revert to the primeval chaos. And yet everything could be so simple."

A woman's shrieks split the night; they came from a shuttered house. Unreal shrieks, dry, without tears. "It's two o'clock," Pedro said without looking at his watch. At his friend's astonishment he explained: "Omar's beating his wife. He does it every night. At two o'clock he gets up and thrashes her. Then he takes her and covers her with love."

"We must do something," Michael protested. "Stop him beating her. It's awful."

"I tried. I talked to Omar. He promised me not to touch her. The next day his wife came and begged me to lift the ban. 'He doesn't love me the same way now,' she complained. 'It's a flabby, weak love. I like him violent! I want him to beat me!' You understand: they love each other. She's screaming; therefore all is well."

"I don't understand that kind of love," Michael said.

"You don't understand love."

"And you? Do you?"

Pedro retreated within himself. The secret, Michael thought. The danger zone. Be careful. They went on walking, and emerged at a spot where the sea lay before them, crystal blue. Pedro stared off into the distance and said, "I've loved. I called her Felicità, though it wasn't her real name. She was a passionate Communist, and fought like a lioness in the Spanish war. She was wounded near Madrid and taken prisoner by the Fascists. Franco's Moors raped her thirty-seven times. I know; a friend of ours who was also wounded saw the whole thing. He counted. Thirty-seven times. She was already dead and they were still spreading her legs and pouring their filth and evil into her. I went mad for weeks, running from one friend to another and shouting, 'I want to die, I want to die!' You understand: I'm Spanish. We don't think about love without thinking about death: I loved and I wanted to die. Love and death: the two most simple things given to man. You asked if I understand love: I understand it because I understand death too."

The sea growled like a wild beast conscious of its power. The previous night an old man had drowned near the port: Michael thought he could hear the groans. He expected Pedro to turn suddenly and suggest, "Come on. Let's drown ourselves." And Pedro did turn to him, but it was to ask a question:

"What would you have done?"

Michael felt himself enlarge. His head touched the heavens and his feet covered the earth: the sea was only a tear gleaming in his right eye. A multitude of faces and destinies waged ruthless battle in his breast: Moishe the Madman was forcing Mendele to drink his urine, Martha was running after Kalman to rape him, Milika was beating old Varady.

"What would I have done?" Michael thundered. "I'd have shaken the universe!" His words echoed above the booming of the sea. Michael clenched his fists. The storm roared within him. "I'd have found Felicità's body," he went on. "I'd have dug up every body in Spain until I found it. And then I would have made love." Michael had to fight to keep his knees from buckling, to keep from dashing to join the waves and the man they had swallowed up the night before.

"You frighten me," Pedro said. "You want to eliminate suffering by pushing it to its extreme: to madness. To say 'I suffer, therefore I am' is to become the enemy of man. What you must say is 'I suffer, therefore you are.' Camus wrote somewhere that to protest against a universe of unhappiness you had to create happiness. That's an arrow pointing the way: it leads to another human being. And not via absurdity."

Of all the words Michael ever heard Pedro speak, these were later the ones that came to his aid.

* * *

The week was almost over. Again Michael set about preparing for his departure. The newspaper in Paris had informed him that his articles were satisfactory: they would run, the public was eager for more.

"What can I do for you?" Pedro asked.

"Nothing. You've already done enough."

They were getting drunk on black coffee in Michael's room. A small lamp glowed on the night table, plunging the rest of the room into a gentle half-shadow. The city was asleep. Pedro was smoking his pipe. Michael thought that he would be in Casablanca the next day. Will I ever see my friend again? His heart contracted.

"Tell me, Michael, if an angel asked you to make one wish, what would it be?"

Michael thought it over at length, and then answered with a sad smile, "To see my home town one last time. I'd cheerfully give ten years of my life to spend twenty-four hours there."

"What for?"

"To see. To see what's become of the city while I was away. A little as though a dead man were able to come back to earth the day after his funeral. To see his friends, and his enemies, who go on living, fighting, cheating as though he'd never existed." He stood up, and paced the room. Pedro watched him, legs crossed, smiling calmly. "Since the end of the war," Michael went on, "all I've done is search for Szerencseváros. I thought it might be anywhere except where geography said it was. I told myself that the city too had been deported, transplanted, to Germany or to heaven. Now I'd like to go back. To see if it exists, if it's still what it was." He couldn't stand still. He burned with it: "You've heard of the wise men in India who get up one morning and leave their wives and children to go off to search for the truth without even knowing where it may be found? I know where: in Szerencseváros."

Pedro poured himself another cup of coffee, drank a few mouthfuls slowly, lit his pipe again, and seemed amused. "So that's your wish?"

"Yes."

"Well, it's feasible."

"What's feasible?"

"A quick trip to Hungary."

"You're crazy!"

"Not at all. You forget that I have a certain organization at my service. It extends to central Europe too. We keep up regular contacts with Hungary. Our men come and go. Nothing's impossible for us; we're the postwar angels. Thick as the Iron Curtain is, we've cut holes through it."

In mounting excitement Michael stood before Pedro, who was smoking calmly, seemingly detached, his eyes sparkling maliciously.

"You're not fooling me, Pedro?"

"Not in the least."

"You can really get me into Hungary?"

"Certainly."

"And . . . get me out again?"

"Certainly."

"Impossible! Do it, Pedro, do it for me! As soon as you can! Tomorrow! I'll drop everything, forget about everything else: I'm ready!"

Pedro laughed heartily. "Hold on! Not so fast. It requires certain preparations; very detailed preparations, too."

"How long would it take?"

"A few weeks, a few months."

Michael did not conceal his disappointment; it had been only a dream. He made a gesture of defeat. His mouth tightened bitterly.

"Come on, now," Pedro teased. "Courage, Michael!" Then, seriously, "You'll go to Hungary. I promise you that. Here's what I suggest: go on to Casa, go back to Paris. Wait for a call from me. Don't worry about anything: I won't forget. When the time comes I'll let you know."

Michael resigned himself. To wait: it was what he hated most. To wait for day, wait for night, wait for good weather. "I'll be patient," he promised.

"I don't think so," Pedro said, laughing.

Toward midnight Vassili and Luis showed up. The others couldn't make it; an urgent job kept them away. Vassili pulled a bottle of vodka from his pocket and passed it around.

"We'll drink to impatience," Pedro said.

The four of them finished the bottle quickly. They were all in a melancholy mood. Vassili sang a Romanian *doina,* almost whispering; Luis countered with a Portuguese *fado.* Michael, his eyes shut, sang *Szól a kakas már,* the shepherd's song that the Rabbi of Kalev had ransomed from exile. He saw himself again in Szerencseváros, alone with Moishe the Madman. "You'll never forget me."

Vassili and Luis left shortly afterward. They shook his hand and looked him in the eye, in the manner of men who do not know if they will ever meet again. "When the day comes that the world presses you too hard," Vassili said, "come back to us. You'll always find vodka and good stories."

"It's a promise," Michael said.

Alone again with Pedro he felt very sad.

"Tell me about your town," Pedro said.

"Szerencseváros means the city of luck. Don't make fun of it; I was born there." He poured out memories. He talked about his childhood, as if he were compelled to transfuse to his friend the images and dreams of his past. He spoke of his parents, of the cursed legend of Varady, of Moishe the Madman, of Kalman, of his friends Hersh-Leib and Menashe, whose ambitions were on a Messianic scale.

Puffing at his pipe, Pedro listened. His sensitive face changed constantly, displaying horror, surprise, recognition, anger; most of all, pride. His eyes darkened, deepened, burned brighter; every word changed them. Only mystics are capable of listening with such sustained intensity. Nothing of what Michael said was lost in transmission.

Here and there Pedro interjected "What a city!" or "That's fantastic!" Or again, "I envy you knowing all those legends, coming in contact with all those lives!"

"I give them to you," Michael answered. "They're yours. I make you a gift of my past, Pedro."

Pedro listened. He made the right comment on each episode; and each comment, instead of finishing the story, served to inspire a new one. Michael realized that thanks to his friend he understood his own past better than before. Sometimes Pedro burst out laughing although the story was heart-rending; Michael was not offended. On the contrary. He knew that on a certain level there was a direct link between the story and his friend's laughter. In the same way it happened that Pedro suffered openly though the story he was hearing implied no sadness. There again Michael knew that carried far enough his story led to blood in the streets. To know when to cry and when to laugh one has only to see far enough ahead. And Pedro's strength was precisely that: he saw far ahead.

Toward six in the morning Pedro stood up and invited him for a last stroll. The air was cool. A sea wind announced the approach of winter. Night was preparing to desert the city. Neither Michael nor Pedro noticed the cold. They walked side by side, silent, together in the day about to dawn.

They went back to the hotel, had another cup of coffee, and proceeded to the station. In the car Pedro remarked, "I won't forget last night. From now on you can say 'I am Pedro,' and I, 'I am Michael.'"

Michael, too moved, didn't answer. Neither would he forget that night; it would keep him company later on.

They had a few minutes at the station. His brow furrowed, Pedro set his heavy hands on his friend's shoulders, as if to anoint him, and said, "Try to help others. Many others. Obviously it isn't the number that matters. But then again, how can you help one man and not another? The silent walk side by side— that's what men must discover. I know: it's impossible and contradictory. But at least let no man reject the chance. In rejecting, a man rejects himself; he isolates us all, and himself too."

"Will we meet again, Pedro?"

"Maybe, little brother. But that's not important. Not any more. As a parting gift I offer you these lines from Plato: 'who . . . sees the beauty of the earth is transported with the recollection of the true beauty; he would like to fly away, but he cannot; he is like a bird fluttering and looking upward and careless of the world below.' Do you see? Whether or not we meet again isn't really very important."

Later on there were trips by night, whisperings in the dark, furtive meetings with strangers barely glimpsed, risky, silent waiting; to pierce the Iron Curtain was by no means an easy enterprise. Death was at hand, within reach: an informer at the hotel, a spy of innocent aspect, a sentry with a submachine gun in his fist, a dog nosing the wind. The longest mile in Europe was there, at the border. Often men and women put all their lives in play to cross it; and died before reaching the goal.

"Why did you come?" Michael asked.

"I've never visited Hungary."

Michael had not expected to see him again. In the telegram from Tangier he had found only instructions for making contact with the agent: first-class compartment, car number 761. When he opened the door, eager to see the man at whose side he would brave risks and dangers, he was struck dumb.

"Good morning, Michael. Going away?"

"You . . . you . . ." the young man stammered.

Pedro was sublimely calm, as if he had just got off a good joke. He was smoking, and seemed contented, amused, comfortable.

"I didn't know," Michael said. "I had no idea it would be you."

"I like surprises," Pedro said nonchalantly.

There were tears in Michael's eyes. He had never felt as close to anyone. He would have liked to do something for him. Offer him a precious object. Suffer for him. Die for him. "Thank you, Pedro," he murmured.

"You're welcome. There's nothing more pleasant than to surprise a little brother. If you could have seen yourself, framed in the doorway, you would have believed in the richness of existence—as I do—in the possibility of having it and sharing it. It's so simple! You see a musician in the street; you give him a thousand francs instead of ten; he'll believe in God. You see a woman weeping; smile at her tenderly, even if you don't know her; she'll believe in you. You see a forsaken old man; open your heart to him, and he'll believe in himself. You will have surprised them. Thanks to you, they will have trembled, and everything around them will vibrate. Blessed is he capable of surprising and being surprised. If I had a prayer to address to God, it would be, 'O God, surprise me. Bless me or damn me: but let thy benediction or thy punishment be a surprise.'"

Only the two of them in the compartment. Pedro was bright, alive, as if he were leaving for a vacation. No sign of nervousness, no gesture betraying uneasiness. Michael examined him more closely: he was thinner. His face was more gaunt, his complexion paler. But his eyes had lost none of their fire, their power.

"You shouldn't have come," Michael said.

"Why not? I've always wanted to learn something about Hungary, and particularly about that town called . . . what's it called again?"

"Szerencseváros, Pedro. Szerencseváros, the city of luck."

"That's it. I wanted to find out if it really brings luck. The only way is to go there."

Michael thought, you shouldn't have come, but I'm glad you're here. Together, we'll win. When two solitudes unite, there is the world on the one hand, and they on the other—and they are stronger than the world. More solid. More real.

The train clacked eastward. Landscapes fled past the window. Pedro chattered away and Michael thought: He's talking too much. He never talked so much before. He has a presentiment. When you can't stand silence it's usually because you want to stifle a voice. What is it saying to him? What voice is it?

Frozen under a driving rain, the two friends and their guide lay prone in a trench. They had been told to take up that position at eleven at night and hold it until three in the morning. The guide from the other side would reach them then. If anything went wrong the attempt was to be set back two days, for four o'clock. Luckily there was no rain the second time.

Pedro gave Michael his last instructions: "On the other side we separate. There'll be two men, one for each of us. Yours is called Miklos. He'll escort you right into the city. You've got three days. Rendezvous: six in the evening. Where do you want to wait for us? Tell me a suitable place."

"Across from the station," Michael said. "Across from the smaller station. There are two, a big one and a small one. I'll wait across from the small one."

"No," Pedro said. "Stations are generally watched."

"In front of the old cemetery, then. The street's not much used."

Pedro weighed the idea, assented: "All right. The old cemetery. My guide will find it. Where will you stay for the three days? Have you got friends you're sure of?"

"I think so. Dr. Todor was my father's closest friend. He won't denounce me."

"And if the doctor won't do it?"

"Then I'll sleep in old Martha's wooden shack. It must be empty. Martha must have died a long time ago."

The guide shushed them. They could hear the sentries on the other side. The night was cloudy, the darkness thick. Another half hour. Michael felt feverish. The great adventure. The road back. Soon he would see himself, know himself, compare himself.

"In case you're arrested," Pedro added, "try to hold out three days. Enough time for the guides to cross the border or disappear. Are you afraid of pain?"

"I think I am."

"They don't torture in their prisons. I hear they've invented a new system: they drive the prisoner crazy. They lock him up in a cell called 'the temple' and keep him standing face-to-the-wall for hours, for days. They call it 'the prayer.' Do you think you can hold out for three days?"

"I'll try."

Pedro dropped a hand to his shoulder.

The guide repeated his order for silence. Five minutes more. Total night. The air grew heavier, fuller. His heart pounding violently, Michael had to grit his teeth to keep his breathing quiet. Valéry: one must attempt to live. Nietzsche: one must live dangerously. The Bible: and ye shall choose life. Two minutes. Possible to back down? To say no? Too late. It had been too late even in Paris. It had been too late even in Tangier. If he had not met Pedro . . . but he had met him. Pedro: the perfect friend, the clear-headed man who loved dignity. Love and death. Friendship and childhood. One minute. The guide reared up, still hugging the damp ground with his legs. Far off, the barking of a dog. Zarathustra: man is a rope over an abyss. No: man is a cord between birth and death, therefore over two pits. When birth unites with death, the cord disappears. Thirty seconds. Ready? Ready. A low buzzing. Someone: "Hssst." Once more: "Hssst." And a third time: "Hssst." The signal. Foward now. Quickly Michael squeezed his friend's arm: a farewell gesture. God of my childhood, show me the way that leads to myself.

Someone was speaking to him. A sad, human voice. He could not make out the words. A fog blanketed them. He tried to open his eyes. He succeeded after an effort that left him sweating. Pedro had disappeared. The guides had disappeared. Only the wall was there. And the voice had a human note, a sad note.

"Come closer. I know it's hard. But don't be discouraged. Gently. Gen-tly. The right leg. The left. About face. There. Like that. Once again. Keep it up."

The third officer was young and agreeable. Seated behind the wooden table, he observed, and a deep sympathy was reflected in his thin, tormented face.

"Come closer," he said. "Don't be afraid."

Without raising his legs Michael shuffled toward him. It made a remarkable racket. He was terribly heavy, weighed down by a nightmare.

"Sit down," the officer said. "Rest."

In the attempt to sit Michael choked back a shriek of pain: his knees were cracking like kindling. Finally he managed to seat himself on a backless chair, his legs stretched almost horizontal before him.

"I don't like this job," the officer confided. "I'm not made to be a jailer or a torturer. Like you, I'm a writer. I studied literature in Budapest. I dreamed of becoming a poet. Putting everything into words, into music, up to and including silence. Seizing the moment and stripping it bare. Explaining man to man. Unfortunately the government had no use for poets. It needs jailers and torturers: they make people sing. Poets are crushed to the wall. Would you like a cigarette?"

His throat dry, his gullet aflame, Michael shook his head, no. He saw himself buried alive in scorching desert sands: only his head emerged to glow in the sunlight.

"Does it surprise you that I talk this way? What else can I do? Silence oppresses me, too. Whom can I talk to, confide in? My colleagues? They'd turn me in. Only here, in 'the temple,' in the heart of the prison, can I feel secure and free. Someone like you knows how to keep his mouth shut. Someday I'll write a great poem on the prisoners of silence. Someday . . ."

Michael thought: this is a trap. You want to rope me in with sympathy and kindness. But I won't fall for it. You're shrewd: you seem to open yourself, to win men over. Thanks a lot, but it's no go. Soon you'll be asking me questions that seem quite innocent. If I know Petöfi Sándor's work, for example. I won't answer. The next question would be, don't I have a message I'd like to get to my friends outside? No. No message. I have no friends.

"One day," the officer said dreamily, "I'll be sitting across from someone like you and we'll be talking about literature and art. There'll be no distrust between us. The gaps will be bridged. We'll be able to look each other in the eye without afterthoughts. Everything will be frank and open."

Keep talking, Michael thought. Go on. I'm naïve, but not to that point. You do it well, anyway. Your buddies—the tough ones—laid the groundwork for you: "They're disgusting, but I'm goodhearted and understanding; I'm your friend." Well, no. It won't wash. I know those tricks.

". . . I know you don't trust me. I can read your thoughts. Saint-Exupéry talks somewhere about the silences of the desert, and he lists them. He might have compared them to the silences of a prisoner. Infinite in number. Angry silence, calm, hateful, resigned, confident, distrustful, rebellious, despairing, mocking, humiliated, humiliating. I'm getting to know them. I don't know what you're thinking, but I know how you're thinking it: in a major key or a minor key. I can distinguish the tone, the color, the climate of your thoughts. Admit that you don't trust me, that I hardly inspire confidence. But you're wrong. Notice: I don't distrust you."

With good reason! Michael thought. Let's not change places. One of us is a prisoner, the other a jailer. There's a bond between us, yes. We're part of the same world, we speak the same language. But let's not carry things too far. If anyone risks paying a price for every word, it's me, it's my friend, and not you. So go ahead. Knock yourself out. Play your part right to the end.

The officer leaned forward as if to accentuate each word with his body: "Trust me, please. I'm not your enemy."

Easily said, Michael thought. You're not my enemy, but you're torturing me. My pain is welded to you: it's you who turn the screw. You tighten it a little more, a little less. You're not my enemy! That's funny!

Suddenly they heard footsteps in the corridor, slow, inexorable. The terrified officer glanced about wildly, like a thief taken in the act. "Get up," he whispered. "Quick, quick, I tell you! They'll get me for this! Get up! You've got to! Get back against the wall!"

The steps in the corridor echoed louder. The next scene begins, Michael thought. He tried to get up; he failed miserably. His body refused to obey him. His legs were no longer wood, but cotton; his flesh was disintegrating. He tried to push himself up on his arms, but they wouldn't support him; they belonged to someone else. In a last effort he managed to lurch forward. He crashed to the floor. The officer leaped to his side and pulled him to the wall by his legs. There he let him drop.

At that moment the door opened and the colonel appeared. The officer saluted: "The prisoner has just passed out! This very moment!"

"Try to bring him around."

The officer knelt and slapped the inert face several times. Michael showed no sign of life. The slaps grew more violent, with no result.

"The idiot," said the colonel. "Keeping his mouth shut, playing hero, when he has nothing to tell us anyway. A fool! Have him taken downstairs and thrown into a cell."

Two guards picked Michael up by the legs and shoulders and carried him out. The colonel blew his nose, but delicately; the colonel had very fine manners.

The Last Prayer

A SAD-FACED MAN WAS SHAKING HIM FRANTICALLY.

Slowly Michael regained consciousness. I'm alive, I hurt, I'm nauseated.

"Did you bring me the letter?"

He half-opened his eyes. "Where am I?"

"Did you bring me the letter?" the man repeated.

"How long have I been here?"

He had to move himself back into time. He opened his eyes wide. Lying on his back. A face above him, the face of a vulture, spying on him, raising his shoulders, letting him fall back.

"Where's my letter?"

"What letter?" Michael asked.

"Don't play dumb. You know what letter. The one I'm waiting for. The one that never comes. The one they're hiding from me. They won't give it to me. Where is it? Don't you have it?"

Michael understood not a word of this. He made an effort to orient himself, to restore some identity to himself, situate himself. The temple, the prayers, the officers, the wall: how long ago had he left them?

"You don't have it? You really don't have it?" the man pleaded.

"No, I don't have it."

The other was motionless for an instant, as if judging the truth of the answer. Then with a vague, weary gesture he got up and went back to his corner. Rolling over to lean on his elbows, Michael glanced around the cell: there were three other prisoners. All filthy. Several weeks' growth of beard. Each of them occupied a corner. He himself was near the door, across from the man who had been shaking him. Near the window a very handsome Jew, with the moving face of a Byzantine Christ, was murmuring prayers. A young man, almost a child, was across from him: he stared straight ahead, seeming at once intent and distraught. Michael spoke to the Jew: "How long have I been here?"

"A few days."

"Are you sure?"

"As sure as one can be."

Michael released a sigh: "I saved him."

"Who's that?" the Jew asked.

"A friend."

He imagined Pedro, already far off: in Austria. Perhaps Paris. Or even Tangier, at the Black Cat. He must have come to the meeting place and waited awhile, probably an hour. Then he'd understood and got out.

"You're happy," the Jew said.

"How can you tell?"

"By your eyes: they glow."

Michael frowned and said nothing. The other went on: "Keep that taste of happiness in your mouth, keep that vision of a friend saved in your eyes. Cling to them. They'll be useful to you. They'll help you not to surrender."

Michael was about to ask, "Surrender to what?" but

the other gave him no time; he had already continued the thought: "Not to surrender to the breakdown of sanity, of your person, of your soul. In a word, to madness."

The Jew came to sit beside him, back-to-the-wall. He introduced himself: Menachem. From Marmaroszighet. "And you?" Michael, born in Szerencseváros. "Right here?" Yes, right here. Yes, that happens: you go back home, you think you're opening the door to the old family home, and it's the door of a prison, or an insane asylum.

"Are you guilty?"

"Of what?"

"Of anything. I hope you are. It's harder for the innocent."

Mistrustful, Michael left the remark hanging.

"Did they make you say your prayers?" Menachem asked.

"Yes."

"How long did it last?"

"I can't really remember. I think three times eight hours, maybe a little less. I remember hearing the voices of three different duty officers."

Menachem stiffened, his gaze intense: "And God's?"

Michael did not understand: "God's? What do you mean?"

"You didn't hear the voice of God?"

Menachem's dark face fairly burned with kindness and warmth. Dressed like a barefoot beggar, he resembled one of those saints who choose exile in order to purify the soul by stripping it of all attachment to the earth.

"No," Michael said. "It never got through to me. The walls must have been too thick."

Menachem nodded pensively: Yes, I understand. Sometimes the walls are too thick. But you erected them with your own hands. "*I* heard his voice," he said. "It asked me questions and gave me the answers. Thanks to that, I held out; I wasn't alone."

"Neither was I," said Michael.

Menachem broke off his nodding. He stared at Michael as if at a madman. He waited, alert.

"My friend kept me company," Michael said. "Not God: my friend. And don't tell me that God sent him."

"I won't say that. God doesn't send people to prisons; he goes himself."

"He may have been busy that day," Michael said ironically. "No doubt he had other cells to visit."

The Jew's face blazed with active, painful suffering. He bit his swollen lips. He searched for the right answer.

"Don't blaspheme," he chanted. "All is not madness. God is not madness. What do we know of God or madness? Of the origin of the act? Our knowledge is limited, negative. When God asked Job, 'Where wast thou when I laid the foundations of the earth?' Job knew not how to answer. He submitted. Better: he returned his mind to God, so that the reflection could merge again with the source of light. Trust your intelligence to God; he will restore it to you intact, if not purer, more profound."

Menachem subsided. Huge transparent tears flowed from his eyes. The last door that closes in heaven, the very last, is that of tears. Michael remembered the rabbi who had raised his cup at a holiday festival and cried out "God is joy!" and then burst into tears. God is joy and Menachem was weeping tears clear as crystal.

"Why are you crying?" Michael asked gently.

"These trials must have some meaning. But sometimes they're so hard that their significance escapes us. And then I wonder: why does God insist that we come to him by the hardest road?"

"Why, Menachem? Do you know?"

"Alas, no!"

"So?"

"I say to God: what do you want of me? I am weak, small, and vulnerable. You are great, powerful, invincible. Do you set me a question? Withdraw it. I do not know how to answer it. I only know how to weep. You have taught me only to weep." He looked up, but his voice dropped: "Pray, Michael. It's your only chance. Pray to God to open the source of tears within you."

Michael shook his head: "Never."

Menachem sighed a sigh of timeless melancholy: "You're headed straight for perdition."

"That's possible. But I prefer to go down laughing."

"Laughing?" Menachem stared at him for a moment, motionless, and then retreated to his corner beneath the window. There he set to praying again. After a time he interrupted himself and spoke to Michael again, in the same prayerful intonation: "Words, Michael, are a double-edged sword. To some they bring light, from others they withdraw it. They urge some to salvation, and others to ruin. It is through the word that God created the universe, and it is by the word that man is destroying it. There is mystery in words, Michael. But we do not know how or why we say certain things, express certain images, in a certain way. We extract words from the deepest recesses of our being. What binds one word to another is no less mysterious than what binds one human being to another. The latter can describe his troubles in a dozen different ways. All the experience of his consciousness, all the experience of his ancestors, help him to make his choice. A thousand generations come to his aid every time he hesitates, for a fraction of a second, between 'the child trembled' and 'the child shuddered.' You need a lot of courage, Michael, a lot of courage to give up that adventure, to accept prayers ready-made and to repeat them day after day. Maintain that courage. If not, you will not hold out. Look at our two companions: they didn't hold out."

The silent man was staring off into space. The other was fumbling in his pockets in search of the imaginary letter.

Michael wondered: is Menachem crazy too? Some, like Spinoza, are God-intoxicated. Others, like the prophets, are God-demented. And Menachem? Not intoxicated, no. But demented? Why not? How is Menachem different? "God is not madness," he had said. Who knows? And if, after all, He were? That would explain so much.

"Listen to me, Pedro. Listen."

"I'm listening," he said, with his intelligent smile.

"I have to tell you what happened. I have to."

"Go on."

He tilts his head to the right, as always when he listens attentively. He isn't smoking. Where's his pipe? Upstairs, probably. Pedro without his pipe seems different: armless. Do the others in this cell see him? Certainly not. If they do, they're pretending not to. Menachem is praying, rocking back and forth. The mute is still drinking in the emptiness around him, his mouth open. The third, the one across from me, is scrabbling at the floor on all fours: looking for the letter. Perhaps Pedro sees them, but is pretending not to notice. And I? Do I see Pedro? Do I really see him? Is it Pedro? Pedro, are you here?

"Of course I am. Where do you think I'd be?"

"Are you listening to me?"

"Of course."

We got to town in the morning, Miklos and I.

We got to town in the morning. The car dropped us at the gates of the city. Miklos gave me money and told me we would go our separate ways: two strangers would inevitably attract attention. Rendezvous in three days at the cemetery.

It was morning, a morning in autumn. The weather was fine. A yellowish sun—old, worn—crept cautiously across a gray sky. Yellow, the foliage; yellow, the walls of the houses; yellow, the dead leaves; yellow, sad, discouraged, the men and women on their way to work.

I looked into the eyes of the people I passed: will I recognize someone? A friend, an enemy? Never saw them before. Strangers. A fear engulfed me: am I really in Szerencseváros, the city of my birth? I know these buildings, I remember the color of the sky, blue-green on the horizon and above the bleak mountains. But I do not recognize the people. A stranger in my own city, where I first saw my mother—where I first discovered the laws of gravity.

Mother had taken me in her arms and was playing in front of a mirror with me. It took me a good hour to realize that the image was myself; I burst into tears. I was there, in the mirror! I began to laugh: the joy of not being alone, of belonging, of being bound to someone, to someone who had lived before me and was living outside me.

And here I am alone. Mother is no more. The mirror harbors other visitors: the mirror itself would reject me and deny me.

Suddenly a long-forgotten episode returned to my mind. I must have been about nine years old. Father had just come back from a trip. Late on a winter afternoon. He took off his fur-collared overcoat, presented me with my gifts, and disappeared into the other room with Mother, closing the door. I was unhappy. They didn't share things with me. They were abandoning me, excluding me. I left the house for spite and went out into the street, into the snow. I wished for death. I wished my death to spite them. That same evening I fell sick. Pneumonia. Temperature 104°. For three days I wavered between life and death. Father and Mother never left my bedside. They didn't even go to the store. They didn't go off to lock themselves in their room.

Was that why I had insisted on coming back? To retrieve memories, my childhood? My first disillusionments, my first anguishes, my first desires for extinction?

I turned down Kamar *utcza*. My cousin lived across from the barracks. Now and then I visited him with Mother. I was afraid of the barracks: they spent two years there, two years far from their friends, separated from their families. "Don't be afraid, my son," Mother told me. "Before you're old enough for military service the Messiah will come." Well, the Messiah hasn't come, I've reached the age of military service, and I've never yet set foot in that barracks.

Mother believed firmly in the imminent arrival of the Messiah. She told me often that the celebrated Rabbi Moishe of Uhel never went to bed without laying out his holiday clothes on a chair: should he be awakened at night to greet the Messiah, he would lose no time in putting on his festive finery. The rabbi is dead, Mother is dead: the Messiah has not come.

I pass before the Villa Gabriel. I remember Gabriel. A disquieting character of distinguished aspect, elegant, breathing scorn. He strolled about with a silver-knobbed ebony cane. The Jews did not offer him a greeting, and stepped off the sidewalk sooner than brush against him. They seemed to fear physical contact, as if he might contaminate them. He was a renegade. In love with a Hungarian girl, he had embraced the Catholic faith and married her. No Jew had spoken to him since. Later he became a lonely widower. The priest, all in black and big-bellied, was his only companion. The other Christians, the true Christians and the others, the Christian-born, had not taken him in: in their eyes he remained a foreigner, an intruder, the Jew who had denied his people not for love of the truth, but only for love: clearly insufficient reason. But the priest demonstrated better proofs of charity. He came often to the Villa Gabriel; and the food was good.

Gabriel the apostate and the priest with the hungry mouth . . . what had they to say to each other during the long winter evenings, the interminable winter evenings when the mountain gales screamed like a thousand hounds in the face of death? Did they speak of religion, of Moses, or Jesus; of their plundered, wasted heritage? Were they frank with each other? Did they tell each other all, really all?

One day Gabriel returned to his people: he appeared in the ghetto, still very erect, elegant, radiating distinction. In his hand was a leather briefcase, his only baggage. It was all that remained of the villa, of his fortune. A Jewish official asked him, "Were you forced to leave your home?" Gabriel reddened and kept silent. He had returned voluntarily to share the fate of his brothers—who spat as he passed.

The villa is now occupied—as I shortly learned—by the secret police, which has there installed its own offices and altars.

I walk down Kamar *utcza*. At the corner of Kigyo *utcza* is our house. Correction: my house. Correction: the house. Blood beats in my temples. My head is a drum: a thousand and one throbbings within. Here is number 27. Then 23, 21, 19. Across the street, the rabbi's home; it now quarters a company of cavalry.

Kamar Street, Number 17. My home and my haven was there. The house is still there, but it is no longer a haven. And yet seen from the outside it has not changed.

There is the store. Already open. Father too opened very early. Mechanically I ascend the two steps and enter. No one. I hear footsteps from the direction of the apartment. I am suddenly overwhelmed by an enormous, incomprehensible, dark fear: my father's footsteps! What would I do if it were he? I need air.

My father is dead, Pedro. I saw him die. I was with him right to the end. Or almost. As far as the threshold. But just the same: if it was only a dream? If he had just pretended to die? To leave? If he were dead only in my dream? If it were he approaching? I was frightened half to death.

Pedro leaned toward me, bending forward sharply: "Is that why you went back? To convince yourself that your father is really dead?"

I ignored his question. I proceeded. A man of about fifty appeared.

A man of about fifty appeared. He was not surprised to see me, and simply asked me what I wanted to buy. I didn't answer immediately. Was this my father? Was that my father's voice? No, a strange face, a strange voice. And yet I wasn't sure, wasn't convinced, not absolutely sure and convinced. My father might have changed; I might have changed; my eyes and ears might have changed. Or suppose I'd forgotten what he was really like?

That fear wasn't new. I remember: I had gone to the station to meet my father on his return from Budapest, where he had spent ten weeks in prison, accused of procuring false identity cards for Polish Jews who had managed to escape from the Germans. Mother had to stay at the store. She'd sent me to meet my father. Heralded by a cloud of black smoke, the locomotive puffed into the station. I was about to see my father again, but a childish distress swept over me: would I recognize him? Had he remained constant to my memory of him? What is a memory? An illusion. Whence the terror of passing by without recognizing him.

The man wiped his hands on his gray jacket, splotched with oil stains. He looked sleepily out at me from behind his thick-lensed glasses: "What can I do for you, *fiatal úr?*"

For a long moment I didn't move. I stared at him: my father did not wear glasses. And yet his voice came to me, as if from beneath the counter, from the depths of a secret drawer: "What are you doing here? You're too little to be in the store."

Mother: "Leave the boy alone. Don't worry: he'll never be a storekeeper."

Father: "He'll be a philosopher."

Mother: "No. A rabbi."

Their eternal argument: it made them laugh. Laugh: it's your right. I am a clandestine traveler who has come home without even knowing why.

"What can I offer you, *fiatal úr?*" the man repeated, fighting sleep.

"A candle," I stammered. It was the first thing that came to mind.

"A candle? So early in the morning?" He smiled.

"I don't see too well," I answered, grimacing stupidly.

During the interrogation later I had a hard time explaining the candle in my pocket. First the colonel suspected me of having hidden microfilm, military secrets, in it. He sent it right off to the police laboratory, where of course they reported that it did indeed seem to be an ordinary, very innocent, candle—and of mediocre quality at that.

"That's very funny!" the merchant commented.

"You don't see well. . . . That's a good one. Ha, ha, ha!"

When I heard his thick laughter I suddenly wanted to go for broke, to say to him, "I am Michael. This is my store, this is my house. You're living off my store and in my house." Only those few words. Just to see his face, catch his expression. After that, I didn't care. To hell with the rest of it. At least I wouldn't have been a stranger in my own house. But that desire passed immediately. I composed myself, paid, bade him farewell, and left the premises, knowing definitely that this time it was for good.

Walking toward the center of town I wondered: What have I really come here to do? To go calling on a store-keeper? On phantoms? Just to say good-bye—a last good-bye—to the store, to the echoes crowded into it?

It was market day. The streets were swarming with peasants from the nearby villages in their colorful costumes. They were all shouting and gesticulating and bargaining. I yearned to see just one familiar face, to hear just one familiar voice: nothing.

There is the butcher, right across from the church. In my memory he remains a broad-shouldered man whose brute strength seemed to have been infused by his disembowled animals. Now I see him through the window, among slabs of meat hung from the wall on hooks. His face echoes the same red. Is it he? A little older, but is it he? Finally someone who hasn't changed?

Three old women, wrapped in their widow's scarves, opened the little door and entered the church; its façade was reflected in the window. It was as though they had entered the butcher, who was at that moment engaged in yawning, his mouth monstrously wide.

What have I come here to do? To what call had I

responded? Of course there was simple curiosity: to look back. Lot's wife was more human than her husband. She too had wanted to carry with her the image of a city that would live—that would die—without her. Doubtless there was something of that in my need to retrace my steps. But after that? Could that be all? Impossible. If it had been so, I'd have felt it; I'd have been satisfied. I want to see my city again; I saw it. The store: I was in it. The people: there they are. And yet I was certain that I had not accomplished the essential task.

And then I realized that there had been many reasons for my return, but the main one was somehow linked to a precise purpose, to a clear aim. I was looking for something, but did not know what; for someone, but did not know whom.

I left the butcher shop and wandered at random. Perhaps a stone, an inscription, a gesture would help me to know.

The house of Kalman the Cabalist: no. Kalman is dead; Hersh-Leib and Menashe too. The Talmud Torah: a state-owned store. Peasants are waiting in line out front. Inside they no longer dispense the word of God, but oil, flour, toothpaste. The merchants are in the temple: they have driven out the rabbis.

I go back to Szinház *utcza*. I had a friend there, Yanku, a redheaded boy who was fanatical about making the dead speak. Every time a man was buried Yanku rushed to the cemetery that same evening, lit a candle on the fresh grave, and recited formulas he had dug out of an old book. While I admired his courage, I refused to go with him. "The dead know the truth," he said. "That's true," I said, "but theirs is the truth of the dead." Yanku did not give up his nocturnal excursions until one night when he accidentally set a fire in the middle of the cemetery. "It's their work," he explained to me. "They keep their secrets jealously."

A few doors from there lived Todor, my father's friend, one of the important people of the city. Call on him right away? Not yet. Later. I'd have to talk, listen, explain, lament the past. I wasn't up to that. In the evening it would be easier.

I cut through Zsido Street, crossed the Grand-Rue (they called it the Corso: Saturday afternoons boys and girls strolled along it in separate groups, exchanging glances at once timid and conspiratorial), passed the municipal jail, and looked eagerly for the august building of the Great Synagogue, the largest and oldest in the city.

From where I was I should have been able to see it; I saw nothing. My heart pounding, I hurried. I clung to the walls to broaden my horizon. No synagogue in sight. Horribly uneasy, I broke into a trot. Hardly a minute: I stopped short, as though my legs had been sliced off by a scythe. Not a trace of the synagogue. Goggle-eyed, I stared at the site. A new building had replaced the house of prayer. A modern four-story edifice. Three cars in the courtyard. Later I learned from the colonel himself that before evacuating the city the Germans had set fire to the synagogue: for twenty days the smoke had curled above the ruins; crowning them with a strange white aureole: as if prayers, or souls, were rising to heaven, but reluctantly, heartsick.

For a whole hour I prowled about the building, fretting and melancholy, my heart heavy with memories. One Yom Kippur night after prayers Moishe the Madman had had himself tied into a chair opposite the Ark. He glared about him and suddenly shouted, "Strike me, God! Strike at your pleasure! See: I won't defend myself! I'm tied up, so strike if it will please you or bring you honor!" The people laughed and said, "You stay drunk right through Yom Kippur, Moishe!" But that night he had not been drunk.

Memories cascaded through my mind. How many legends had centered on that old synagogue! At night children skirted the building. They said that at midnight the dead came to pray. If they saw someone in the street they called him by name, to come and read the Torah. None had the right to refuse. One night a Jew just getting home heard a voice within: "Get up Isaac, son of Abraham." It was his name. He took fear and ran, frantic, to ask advice of the rabbi who lived next door. The rabbi told him, "If they call you, you must go. You may not insult the dead." Nevertheless, for protection he gave Isaac his rod to hold in one hand and his ritual knife for the other. "Do as I tell you and no evil shall befall you. Enter walking backward, your eyes shut; go up on the dais where we read the Torah; recite the prayer; and when the reading is over go out slowly, very slowly." The Jew followed the rabbi's instructions and survived the experience. Outside again, he found fresh blood on the knife. "It's because you were trembling," the rabbi explained. "By trembling you made them ashamed. In shame, one bleeds."

I came to pray in the Great Synagogue only rarely. I preferred the temple of the Rabbi of Borshe, across the street from us. But twice a year, on the Saturday after New Year's Day and the Saturday before Passover, I went to the Great Synagogue to hear the Grand Rabbi's sermon. He was a young man, handsome, robust, vigorous and severe, and he saw a punishment from God in the suffering of the Jews: that was his favorite theme. God punishes the Jews because he loves them, because he is determined to make them pure and just. In the audience men nodded approvingly while on the floor above, reserved to women, weeping broke out at the first words. Most often they understood nothing of what he said, which did not deter them from weeping copiously and sniffling ardently.

But the real "tear-jerker" was not the Grand Rabbi, but a pathetic soul, uncouth and shabby, whom they called the Rabbi of Csarda after a small village a few miles from Szerencseváros. "They call me the Rabbi of Csarda everywhere except in Csarda," he loved to say. During the High Holidays he always landed a small synagogue where he could officiate as the "messenger of the community" in its dealings with God. What he had was not a beautiful voice, but a broken heart, which is more important and less common. Women loved to hear him speak; he used simple language, current and easily understood images—and tears welled immediately, inexhaustibly.

The last time I saw him he was considerably changed. Beardless, he no longer seemed to be walking on air like someone in a Chagall. He did not have to preach to make people cry: one looked at him and one's eyes filled.

It was right here, at the old synagogue. Yes, I remember now. A Saturday. The police had herded all the city's Jews into the building. The house of prayer and meditation had become a depot where families were separated and friends said farewell. Last stop before boarding the death train.

A memory came to the surface so violently that I felt dizzy.

The window, the curtains, the face: in the house across the way. A spring day, sunny, the day of punishment, day of divorce between good and evil. Here, men and women yoked by misery; there, the face that watched them.

Finally! Everything was clear, stark. There, then, was the reason, the *real* reason, the reason behind all

the other reasons. Relieved, I sighed. Were my acts
and desires obeying an inherent logic? It matters little
if the black night falls once more; it will never again
be the same.

"Are you listening, Pedro?"

"I'm listening, little brother."

"Do you understand me?"

*"I'm listening and I understand. I listen even if I
don't understand; and I understand even if I'm not
listening."*

*Do you understand that I need to understand? To
understand the others—the Other—those who watched
us depart for the unknown; those who observed us,
without emotion, while we became objects—living
sticks of wood—and carefully numbered victims?*

*Pedro bowed his head still lower, as if repentant
and asking forgiveness. Menachem prayed, his eyes
closed. The mute stared at nothing. The third
searched the ceiling: his letter.*

This, this was the thing I had wanted to understand ever since the war. Nothing else. How a human
being can remain indifferent. The executioners I understood; also the victims, though with more difficulty. For the others, all the others, those who were
neither for nor against, those who sprawled in passive
patience, those who told themselves, "The storm will
blow over and everything will be normal again,"
those who thought themselves above the battle, those
who were permanently and merely spectators—all
those were closed to me, incomprehensible.

And as often happens, I saw all those neutrals in
the features of a single face: the spectator across from
the synagogue. The others were only reflections of
him. Copies.

It's because of him that I risked my life—and yours too, Pedro, I know—to come back.

I can still see him, that Saturday. Jews were filling the courtyard. On their backs they carried whatever they had saved of a lifetime of work. Knapsacks into which the old had stuffed their past, the children their future, the rabbis their faith, the sick their exhaustion. The wandering Jew was about to set out again, the exile's staff in his hand. The wandering Jew was headed toward the physical liquidation of his difficulties: toward the "final solution." At last the world was to be relieved of the great problem that had haunted it for two thousand years! Now at last it would be able to breathe!

No one in the crowd was crying. No one wailed or even spoke. Ghosts, thronging up from the depths of history. Fearful, silent ghosts. They awaited the order to move out. Hungarian police, black feathers in their hats, came and went, rifles at the ready, bludgeons poised.

My parents and I stood close to the fence: on the other side were life and liberty, or what men call life and liberty. A few passers-by; they averted their faces; the more sensitive bowed their heads.

It was then that I saw him. A face in the window across the way. The curtains hid the rest of him; only his head was visible. It was like a balloon. Bald, flat nose, wide empty eyes. I watched it for a long time. It was gazing out, reflecting no pity, no pleasure, no shock, not even anger or interest. Impassive, cold, impersonal. The face was indifferent to the spectacle. What? Men are going to die? That's not my fault, is it now? I didn't make the decision. The face is neither Jewish nor anti-Jewish, a simple spectator, that's what it is.

For seven days the great courtyard of the synagogue filled and emptied. He, standing behind the curtains, watched. The police beat women and children; he did not stir. It was no concern of his. He was neither victim nor executioner; a spectator, that's what he was. He wanted to live in peace and quiet.

His face, empty of all expression, followed me for long years. I have forgotten many others; not his. The Hungarian police were cruel. Of them my memory has retained only a vision of detached figures: a mustache, a rifle butt, a gleam of animal joy. And so it is with the Germans: I remember their gestures, their raucous shouts, their icy and methodical brutality. But the only face that my memory has retained intact is his.

I felt neither hate nor anger toward him: simply curiosity. I did not understand him. How can anyone remain a spectator indefinitely? How can anyone continue to embrace the woman he loves, to pray to God with fervor if not faith, to dream of a better tomorrow —after having seen *that*? After having glimpsed the precise line dividing life from death and good from evil?

In Germany I thought of him: what is he doing? Does he sleep well, deeply? Does he eat when he is hungry? Does he remember?

The others, all the others, were he. The third in the triangle. Between victims and executioners there is a mysterious bond; they belong to the same universe; one is the negation of the other. The Germans' logic was clear, comprehensible to the victims. Even evil and madness show a stunted intelligence.

But this is not true of that Other. The spectator is entirely beyond us. He sees without being seen. He is there but unnoticed. The footlights hide him. He never applauds nor hisses; his presence is evasive, and commits him less than his absence might. He says neither yes nor no, and not even maybe. He says nothing. He is there, but he acts as if he were not. Worse: he acts as if the rest of us were not.

It was too early in the afternoon for paying calls; he was surely at work. With nothing better to do I decided to take advantage of the next few hours by exploring the city. I went all the way out to Malomkert, "the garden of the windmills," where people brought children to hear stories about the high deeds of Rozsa Sándor, the famous brigand who had amused himself some centuries earlier by distributing to the poor what he extracted from the rich. They said that one of the nearby caves had been his lair; whoever found it would come into the wealth Sándor had accumulated in the last days before his death; he had had no time to pass it on to his beloved poor.

Some distance from there I ran across old Martha's deserted shack, old Martha who cursed out the children because they threw stones at her. Would she be still alive? The cabin was empty. It had been years since anyone set foot in it. An odor of desolation, of putrefaction, perfumed the air. Martha, the terror of the children, would never curse again. Poor Martha! It was as though she insisted on being hated. Why was she so eager to be detested? Who was she? Had there ever been a time when she was young, beautiful, happy? Had she been born as she was, old, filthy, disgusting? They took her for a witch who slept with Satan. They said she could kill people by reciting a formula that gave her power over natural forces. They also said that she spent her time in the shack transforming sand to gold and good to evil. While she was alive no one had dared cross the doorsill of the shack: they said it was guarded by two black dogs, two ferociously bloodthirsty monsters. Now she is dead. And her cabin empty. The wind itself never even enters.

I went back to Malomkert and sat on the banks of the lake: they were covered with a slimy, dark-green mold.

There, the universe was at rest. The planet no longer whirled. Calm lay upon the spot. No sound reached it from the city. The wind caressed the trees, murmuring secrets to the gilded leaves that they alone understood. Time itself came to a halt, and was a thing that could be examined, questioned, opened. I felt strangely serene, at peace with myself. My whole childhood stretched before me, on the surface of the lake. I was casting up what religious Jews call the *Heshbon Hanefesh*, the accounts of the soul. What had I made of my life? I had suffered and made suffer; I had received and given; hoped and lost hope. And what was left now of one existence? Soon I would be face to face with a man, and would set him those questions, as judge, prosecutor, or spectator. For the game can be played indefinitely: who observes the spectator becomes one. In his turn, he will question me. And which of our two lives will weigh heavier in the balance?

The sun retreated gently down the slope of the afternoon, igniting the clouds that barred its way. The water of the lake darkened, as if elements of the night were already part of it. Leaves rustled. I closed my eyes: sitting on the yellow grass, my back to a tree, I heard a voice call me by name. I looked around and knew that it was not a tree at my back, but my mother. I ask her, "Why have you come back?" She answers, "I was cold." I say, "Come; let's go back to the house." She answers, "I can't; don't you see that I'm a tree?"

My watch tells me it is after six. Time to leave, to go back to the city. On the way I experience a moment of worry: the man no longer lives in the same house! He's no longer alive! I hurry.

Crowded with people going home from work, the streets were like a forest tossed by the wind. They were all hurrying, rushing back to the warmth of the hearth.

I stopped in front of the house. The window was bright. The doorway was in the courtyard. I meditated for an instant: was this really an act of free will? I breathed deeply and pushed at the door without bothering to knock. It was open. In Szerencseváros there was little need to lock doors, even at night. A corridor. At its end, the room that faced the street. In absolute silence I stepped that way. My heart pounded in spite of myself.

There he was.

Seated at a table, leaning on his elbows, his face in profile, he was reading a book. I'd have known him among a thousand. A heavy round head, completely bald. He hadn't changed. But now he was wearing glasses. A symbol of anonymity, the average man. I watched him in silence. A fly skipped along his skull: he didn't take notice. I stared at him without hate, without scorn. All I felt toward him was curiosity.

He sensed a presence suddenly. His eyes shifted toward the door; he saw me and started. "What do you want?"

On his feet, leaning against the table, he faced me. The features I had seen at the window. Large cold eyes, opaque as the ice that covered the river. A startling absence of eyebrows. Receding chin. Innocence itself: what does not exist is by definition innocent.

"I'm thirsty," my little sister said.

"Who are you?"

I did not answer. That was none of his business. I am here: let that be enough. I had no need to define myself in relation to him. I stepped forward, then walked about the room, as if the room interested me far more than his presence. Middle-class furnishings. Heavy, bulky pieces. Even the radio, big as a chest of drawers. On the walls, photographs of a soldier with drooping mustaches: his father, probably. A portrait in enamel, his mother as a girl. Hand beneath her chin, she smiled provocatively.

"*I'm thirsty,*" *my little sister said.*

"Are you from the police?"

He kept his eyes on me. Pale, he was blinking. His lips trembled; he mumbled inaudibly. He took off his glasses to set them on the table, and almost dropped them. I looked again at the enamel portrait: my mother, too, had smiled, but there had been nothing provocative about her. On the contrary: she had been humble, reserved, shy.

She was thirsty, my mother said, but she was embarrassed to mention it.

"You're not from the police!"

He had guessed it from the way I was studying the smile his mother had left behind. The change in his attitude was abrupt. He was no longer afraid. He belonged in the category of people who fear only the police. I was not a policeman; from which it followed that there was no need to be afraid. On top of the radio was a mirror. With my day-old beard I looked gloomy and evil. But not like a policeman.

"What do you want?" he said firmly.

"To humiliate you," I said.

"*I'm thirsty,*" *my little sister said.*

She had the most beautiful hair in the world. The sun loved to carouse in it. But on that spring day—a Saturday—she wore a scarf on her head, as if she were old and a widow. She was eight years old. "*I'm so thirsty,*" *she said.* I couldn't bring her water. The police were guarding the gates of the courtyard. We were forbidden to go out. And this man stood at the window and watched.

"I've come a long way," I said. "I've come to humiliate you."

I wanted to see him on his knees, licking the dust on my shoes. To make him taste the loneliness of cowards. To reduce him to shreds. To deprive him of any picture of himself, to decompose his identity, to scourge pride and self-esteem and countenance from him as one drives children away from a rotting cadaver.

"I'm thirsty," I told him. "Give me some wine."

He lumbered around the table, opened a cabinet, and brought out a bottle of Tokay and two glasses like inverted cones. He set them calmly on the table. I told him to fill the glasses. He did so. The bottle did not tremble in his hand. I took my glass in my right hand. He made as if to do the same. I stopped him. He nodded "All right," and waited. We stared at each other silently. Each gauged the other's strength. He sustained my glare. My fingers curled around the glass with near shattering force. I wanted to shout, "Lower your eyes, you scum! Crawl!" My expression shouted it. He did not give way. His opaque eyes reflected an inner winter, sheathed in ice, impenetrable, stiff. The silence grew heavier. The man betrayed not the slightest sign of weakness. He saw in me an enemy, in this confrontation a duel. Then, in a motion quite abrupt though carefully premeditated, I dashed the wine in his face, which remained impassive. I took the second glass and held it up for him to see: he did not look at it. His eyes never left mine. "Lower them! To the dust!" He received the contents of the second glass with the same calm.

"Fill them," I ordered him.

Without a word he did so again, but his face darkened. When they were full to the brim he pushed the glasses toward me, placing them within my reach.

"Let's talk," I said.

"About what?"

"A Saturday in spring. Nineteen forty-four. On one side, the Jews; on the other, you. Only the window—that window—between."

"I remember."

"With shame?"

"No."

"With remorse?"

"No."

"With sadness?"

"No. With nothing at all. There's no emotion attached to the memory."

I leaned forward slightly: "What did you feel then?"

"Nothing."

The muscles in my face tightened: "Outside, children were sick with thirst: what did you feel?"

"Nothing."

"Outside, men were turning away so as not to see their children doubled up in pain: what did you feel?"

"Nothing." A silence; then: "Absolutely nothing. My wife was crying in the kitchen. Not me. She was sad and miserable. I wasn't." Another silence; then: "No, I tell you. I had a shocked feeling that I was a spectator at some sort of game—a game I didn't understand: a game you had all begun playing, you on one side, the Germans and the police on the other. I had nothing to do with it."

A game! For the first time that evening anger rumbled in me. Because he was right. All the appearances of a game. Of course, we died for real, but that wasn't the point. The way in which we die is what counts. And we went at it as if we were playing a game.

Without protesting, without fighting back, we let ourselves be cast as victims. A revolt, even badly organized, offered fair chances of success: it never broke out. Like a herd of sheep we allowed ourselves to be led. A game indeed! A Greek tragedy in which the characters are condemned in advance, long before the curtain rises. At Szerencseváros, at Marmaroszighet, in a thousand other European cities, the Jews blindly obeyed the implacable instructions of an invisible director. Everywhere the first act was the same, and the second, and the last. A gesture, one only, a shout, one only—some interjection that was not in the script—and everything might have changed: the actors would have reverted to their own identities. That gesture, no one made; that shout, no one shouted. The victims were exemplary victims. Of course, they did not know. They did not know how the story went on, how it ended. They should have known. They could have known. There were a few who knew, who had seen. The others refused to listen to them. The others shut them up. Stopped their mouths. Were ready to stone them. Those were the rules of the game.

"I felt no sadness," the man went on. "I remember: the day after you left, I was walking around in the half-empty city. All your things were strewn in the streets as if the earth had spewed them up. Here and there people were singing and dancing, dead drunk. I didn't touch a thing. It was like being onstage an hour after the end of the show."

The blood beat in my temples. Remorse, shame, anger ebbed and flowed in me. Now I hated him. After all, I was not the defendant here. Even if he was right—and my heart said he was—that didn't justify his spectator's detachment. He too could have interrupted the game. If he had simply gone down to the courtyard of the synagogue and alerted the Jews:

"Good people! Listen to me! Don't be fooled! Be careful! It's not a game!" He hadn't done it.

"Coward!" I shouted, and crashed my fist down on the table. "You're a shameful coward! You haven't got the courage to do either good or evil! The role of spectator suited you to perfection. They killed? You had nothing to do with it. They looted the houses like vultures? You had nothing to do with it. Children were thirsty? You had nothing to do with it. Your conscience is clear. 'Not guilty, your honor!' You're a disgusting coward! You hedge: you want to be on the winning side no matter what! It's easy to say 'I am I and they are they and to hell with them'! It's comfortable to say 'It's all a fraud, they're only playing a game.' And who gave you the right to judge who's playing and who isn't, who's dying and who's just pretending? Who taught you so well to distinguish between suffering and the appearance of suffering?"

I turned my back to him and went to the window, to where he had stood years earlier. In the distance a voice: "Will you be back soon?" I didn't hear the answer. Anyway the ten thousand Jews of Szerencseváros wouldn't be back. Not soon and not late. Not tonight and not tomorrow night. Their role is that of the absent. The favorite role of the dead. As death is the favorite game of the Jews.

There's the audience you performed for, Kalman. And you, Hersh-Leib and Menashe. And you, my little sister. What paltry performers you were! Not a tear in the audience, not a sigh, not a single gasp of horror. Nothing. A thousand times nothing. Martha, the old drunk, did better than you: at least she aroused fear, aroused shame. You—you aroused only indifference. The audience was disappointed. The play provoked no response. Nothing, I tell you. No emotion, no alteration. In the kitchen his wife was crying. But he, front row center, remained dry-eyed and hard-hearted. You played badly! Were you thirsty, little sister? You performed badly. Your thirst was unconvincing.

"You hate me, don't you?"

I turned. His voice had suddenly taken on a human tone. A certain intensity showed in his face.

"No," I said. "I don't hate you." A pause; then: "I feel contempt for you. That's worse. The man who inspires hatred is still human; but not the man who inspires contempt. You don't feel contempt for the executioner; you hate him, and you want him dead. You feel contempt only for cowards. People like you retreat to an ivory tower and say to themselves, 'All the world's a stage and all the men and women merely players. Ah, how pleasant when they make us shiver!' Hatred implies humanity: it has its coordinates, its motifs, its themes, its harmonics. Under certain conditions it can elevate men. But contempt has only one implication: decadence."

He paled perceptibly. His eyes were little more than slits. He stood erect, a hand on his stomach, as though he were sick.

"You won't do it," he said. "You won't humiliate me. You're playing a game, and I won't go along. I refuse to play." He peered at me, and the cold glance grew harder, sharp as a sword: "You accuse me of cowardice. And you? What were you? A few policemen—not more than ten—led you all to the slaughterhouse: why didn't you seize their arms? Can you tell me why?"

"We didn't know," I said tightly. "We didn't know what was ahead of us."

"That's not true! There were some among you who knew, some who tried to warn you; you didn't listen. Why? Why? Can you tell me why you didn't listen?"

"What they were saying sounded too fantastic; nobody could really put much stock in it."

"You were afraid, you preferred the illusion to the bite of conscience, and the game to a show of courage!"

I contained my anger with difficulty. *You were thirsty, little sister.* And he dared to judge you, he, the spectator. This man is accusing you of cowardice. My impulse was to charge him, to blind him, to kill him. A man like that had no right to live and to judge the dead.

"You're right; or rather you may be right. We too could have behaved differently. But you forget that we were victims: they had taken from us not only the right to live—and to drink when we were thirsty—but also any right to clarity. That doesn't apply to you: you weren't a victim. Your duty was clear: you had to choose. To fight us or to help. In the first case I would have hated you; in the second, loved. You never left your window: I have only contempt for you."

My voice was calm. It was important not to hate him. I concentrated my efforts to that end: to silence my hatred. Contempt was what he deserved. Hatred implied something of the human. The spectator has nothing of the human in him: he is a stone in the street, the cadaver of an animal, a pile of dead wood. He is there, he survives us, he is immobile. The spectator reduces himself to the level of an object. He is no longer he, you, or I: he is "it."

He wanted to say something, but I silenced him with a glance. I told him to join me at the window. He did so. We turned our backs to the room and looked out at the courtyard of the synagogue. It must have been close to midnight. The dead would never again come to pray.

"You won't humiliate me," he said.

I ignored his remark and said, "Do you remember the synagogue? Do you think it's destroyed forever?

Wrong. It exists. A synagogue is like the Temple in Jerusalem. The wise men of Israel say that there is one on high and a second here below. The one here below can be reduced to ashes; it's been done twice. But the temple on high remains intact; its enemies cannot touch it. And this synagogue, too, exists. Only it's been transplanted. Every time you raise your eyes you'll see it. And you'll see it so often, so clearly, that you'll pray God to blind you."

"You won't humiliate me," he said.

I ignored him again; I went on, "You think you're living in peace and security, but in reality you're not living at all. People of your kind scuttle along the margins of existence. Far from men, from their struggles, which you no doubt consider stupid and senseless. You tell yourself that it's the only way to survive, to keep your head above water. You're afraid of drowning, so you never embark. You huddle on the beach, at the edge of the sea you fear so much, even to its spray. Let the ships sail without you! Whatever their flag—Communist, Nazi, Tartar, what difference does it make? You tell yourself, 'To link my life to other men's would be to diminish it, to set limits; so why do it?' You cling to your life. It's precious to you. You won't offer it to history or to country or to God. If living in peace means evolving in nothingness, you accept the nothingness. The Jews in the courtyard of the synagogue? Nothing. The shrieks of women gone mad in the cattle cars? Nothing. The silence of thirsty children? Nothing. All that's a game, you tell yourself. A movie! Fiction: seen and forgotten. I tell you, you're a machine for the fabrication of nothingness."

"I will not let myself be humiliated," he said.

And this time too I ignored him and said, "The dead Jews, the women gone mad, the mute children —I'm their messenger. And I tell you they haven't forgotten you. Someday they'll come marching, trampling you, spitting in your face. And at their shouts of contempt you'll pray God to deafen you."

A cool breeze flowed from the window and touched our faces, like the breath of a beast. Stars pursued one another across a very distant sky. A door squeaked. Murmured complaints. Far off the mountains had wrapped their secrets in a heavy cloak.

"I will not let myself be humiliated," the man said.

This time I answered: "Be quiet."

Suddenly I had no further desire to speak or listen. I was weary, as after a battle fought without conviction. I had come, I had seen, I had delivered the message: the wheel had come full circle. The act was consummated. Now I shall go. I shall return to the life they call normal. The past will have been exorcised. I'll live, I'll work, I'll love. I'll take a wife, I'll father a son, I'll fight to protect his future, his future happiness. The task is accomplished. No more concealed wrath, no more disguises. No more double life, lived on two levels. Now I am whole.

"Do you really feel contempt for me?"

I didn't answer. I'd talked enough. Everything had been said. I'll leave Szerencseváros, the city of luck. I'll never come back.

"Come," I said.

We left the window. There was something bizarre about the two glasses of wine on the table.

"Let's drink," I said.

I took a glass and pushed the other across to him. He picked it up hesitantly, not knowing if I would insult him again. The lines around his mouth now revealed bitterness and bewilderment.

"Let's drink to the actors," I said. "To the actors destroyed in their own play."

We clinked glasses, and drained them.

"You don't hate me," he said.

"I told you. I don't hate you."

"But you must!" he cried hopelessly.

"I don't hate you," I said.

"I couldn't bear that! Your contempt would burn at my eyes; they'd never close again! You've got to hate me!"

"No," I said.

He stared at me for a moment and I thought he was going to cry. If he had, I'd have thrown my arms around him. For the first time that night his face had quivered. The veins in his temples were swollen. He ran his tongue around his lips as if to absorb the last drops of wine. Then he smiled a curious, ironic smile, the meaning of which I understood only later.

"I feel sure you'll hate me," he said.

Now his suffering was obvious, as though an unseen hand had engraved it on his skin. He had become human again. Down deep, I thought, man is not only an executioner, not only a victim, not only a spectator: he is all three at once.

It was time to go, I said "Adieu" and without waiting for an answer turned and left, shrugging. The street was empty, asleep. I headed for Dr. Todor's house to see my father's friend. I intended to spend two days there, until the rendezvous.

But no man shouts his scorn and disgust at another with impunity. At the corner of the street running into the main square a car braked sharply at the curb; in the wink of an eye the door opened and two arms flashed out like lightning to drag me inside. In the front seat sat the spectator. I had barely left his house when he was off to warn the policeman on the corner. Our eyes met in the mirror: his were full of defiance, an anticipation of victory, saying, "Now you'll *have* to hate me!"

"*Did you spit in his face?*" Pedro asked.

"*No.*"

"*The man turned you in, and you didn't spit in his face?*"

"*No, my friend. I smiled at him. I smiled at the man to whom I had played God.*"

"*That's crueler,*" Pedro said.

And he rubbed his forehead, absorbed; he always did that when he was moved.

Days and nights flowed by in the gloom that swallowed them up one after another. At first Michael found landmarks in the bread and the soup: bread was distributed in the morning, soup late in the afternoon. But Menachem soon disillusioned him. To confuse their minds the jailers sometimes amused themselves by reversing the schedule. So the prisoners were never quite sure whether it was day or night.

Michael felt his sanity dimming, extinguishing; its flame guttered low. His identity was dissolving in dead time.

Of his three companions, Menachem was the only one with whom he could converse. Naturally he too was touched by madness, but his had at least the virtue of being communicative, possessing its own poetic coherence.

"God is my caretaker," he liked to say. "Under bond I give him all that I am and all that I have: at night, my soul; in the morning, my sanity. In the morning he returns my soul, and he will also restore my sanity."

"I refuse his services," Michael answered. "I'm poor. His prices are too high. I prefer to keep my baggage with me."

The other's handsome, Christlike face radiated compassion: "Don't blaspheme, my friend." He murmured a prayer, leaned forward, and spoke in a very gentle voice: "Are you sure that you are not already mad? Across the line? Are you absolutely convinced that madness wasn't behind your stubbornness? If faith is madness, why can't a lack of faith be the same?"

Not wanting to hurt him, Michael did not answer. One can prove one's sanity only to the sane.

"I grant you, I may be insane," Menachem went on. "It may be that we both are. If we aren't we will be. And yet, Michael, my friend, I prefer to be insane with God—or in Him—than without God, or far from Him."

"Now you're blaspheming," Michael answered.

"There, too, I prefer to blaspheme in God than far from Him."

Thanks to Menachem Michael managed not to founder for some time. When the Jew of Marmaroszighet saw him too sad—or not sad enough—he came over to chat with him, and it was as if he had offered an arm to lean on.

Menachem told him about his own crime against the state: he had organized clandestine classes in religion. At that time anti-Semitism was not only tolerated but encouraged in all countries behind the Iron Curtain. They arrested rabbis and students; they deported them to work camps so that they would not "contaminate" the minds of the young. He, Menachem, was neither a rabbi nor a teacher of religion. He was not even very pious. Often it happened that he transgressed the rigid Sabbath laws, and prayed less than three times a day. The change occurred one afternoon when his little boy came home from school and asked him, "Is it true that the Jews are the cancer of history? That they live off the past? That they invented God just to humble man and stop progress?" Menachem went white beneath his beard. After several months of activity he was arrested. His torturers told him, "We'll make you forget God. You'll not only doubt the possibility of His existence, but also of your own." But he held out. He never ate without covering his head and reciting a prayer over the bread. Even for the daily housecleaning of the cell he had devised a special prayer that he muttered, weeping great tears that brightened his luminous gaze. "You ask me why I cry so much?" he said once. "I'll tell you: to survive. Do you know the story about the king's fool?"

"No, I don't," Michael said without thinking. He might have known it; he knew plenty of stories about kings and fools, playing their parts consciously or not. But he liked to hear his companion's voice. It pulled him out of his stupor.

"One day the king sent for his favorite jester and told him, 'I feel melancholy. I need to laugh. Make me laugh, or you will not see the sun rise again.' Panic-stricken, the fool forgot his art. As if accursed, he could remember no grimace, no dance, no song that normally loosed laughter among the court. Knowing himself doomed, he broke into convulsive sobs. Now, it is well known that fools cannot weep. Their tears are unconvincing; everyone knows they are false tears. As he wept, the fool looked so comical that the king slapped his fat belly and a sufficient roar of laughter escaped him."

"That's a cruel story," Michael said.

"All stories about fools are cruel."

"Are you the fool, Menachem?"

"Maybe."

"Then the king is God. Do you want to make God laugh?"

"God is the king, and I am only a fool. But He is not a king like other kings, and I am not a fool like other fools. All He asks is to weep with us. Within us. For that our tears must remain pure and whole. Their source is the source of life."

"And what lies beyond tears? Do you know?"

"Yes. God. God awaits us beyond all things. Let

yourself go, my friend. Weep and you will find the crust of existence less thick, less hard."

His thoughts far away, Michael smiled: in heaven, near the Celestial Throne, there is a special chalice into which all our tears are poured. When it is full, the Messiah will come. The poet Frug made a song of it, and cried out, "Has that cup no bottom?"

But Menachem never wrung a single tear from his friend. The discussion lasted several days and nights. Michael refused to yield.

One night he woke with a start: he heard strange choking gasps. Michael opened his eyes and was horrified for a moment. The man he had nicknamed "The Impatient One" was strangling the pious Jew. In one bound Michael was upon him, and pushed him back to his corner.

"He's the one who took my letter," the other shouted. "I want it back! I'll kill him!"

Menachem was exhausted. He was rubbing his neck and breathing with difficulty. He seemed sad and distant. Michael knelt beside him, worried.

"Are you all right?" he asked.

"All right."

They were silent for several moments, and then Menachem gave him a look so full of affection that Michael trembled. "Thank you, my friend," Menachem said feebly.

"Be quiet," Michael answered.

He went back to his corner and there, sure of privacy, he wept his first tear. It brought him a sense of relief mingled with shame. A few days later—or was it a few weeks? a few months?—he gave in to it a second time.

It was morning. The guard, entering the cell, bore only three rations of bread. "You," he said to Menachem. "Come with me. You're transferred."

Michael gasped. He had not expected this. He had

never imagined that they might be separated. Through a dream he saw Menachem pick up his blanket, his spoon, and his jacket, an indefinable smile on his lips. Passing Michael, he stopped to embrace him fondly. He repeated the same benediction several times: "God be with you, God be with you!"

"No, Menachem. You'll need him more than I will."

Menachem embraced him tightly and left him abruptly. Michael saw only his back, beyond the doorway; he heard the footsteps trail off in the interminable corridor. He listened closely: nothing more.

Then, so suddenly impoverished, he leaned his head against the wall and broke into sobs, at the end of his tether. Neither the Impatient One nor the Silent One paid any attention. The one searched for his letter, the other no longer sought anything. The Silent One stared fixedly before him, not even noticing that Menachem—the body which for months had filled his field of vision—was no longer there.

Michael felt himself slipping downward. His loneliness grew thicker, heavier. To rise for soup, or to clean the cell, or to urinate in the bucket close at hand, was an almost insurmountable effort. The center of the earth was dragging him down.

Sometimes he tried to remember Pedro, to speak to him, but he felt that his friend was not listening. Cloaked in fog and forgetfulness, Spain was far away, beyond the horizon.

Ah, to do something that one cannot do, that one must not do! To fling oneself beneath a moving automobile, to cut off one's own tongue or ear, to attack one's own sanity, to dig oneself a grave in heaven, an opening in the clouds, and to contemplate oneself in the sun!

Once in an elevator in Paris Michael had stood behind a woman of whom he could see only the nape of the neck. He had no idea whether she was young or old, pretty or homely. Suddenly a thought—a need—crossed his mind: what if I kissed her, right there, on the nape of the neck?

In a bus, another time, his seatmate was a fat burgher who sat twiddling an unlighted cigar. Suddenly Michael hated him. He wanted to shout "You son of a bitch!" and strangle him.

And still another time he was walking down a street when a beggar in a tattered coat got down on his knees to grub for a cigarette butt. Michael felt like lifting him by the collar and asking him, "Why do you hate me? What have I done?"

For Michael madness was a door opening onto a forest, onto the liberty in which anything is permitted, anything is possible. There A does not precede B, children are born dotards, fire produces cold, and snow becomes the source of desire. There, animals are gifted with human intelligence and demons display a sense of humor. There, all is impulse, passion, and chaos. There, the laws are abolished and those who promulgated them removed from office. The universe frees itself from the order in which it was imprisoned. Appearance snaps its ties with reality. A chair is no longer a chair, the king no longer king, the fool ceases to be a fool, or to cry.

To go mad: why not? All he had to do now was adapt to the Impatient One's system: to read him the letter he never ceased calling for. Or to construct a system for himself alone: he would surely not lack ideas. Should he let go? Isn't a bird at the edge of the nest better off beating toward the heights? He'll plummet to earth? So what?

A character from Shakespeare obsessed him: that old man enraged by the neglect of others, who falls to his knees and murmurs despairingly, "O fool, I shall go mad!" There was a man who preferred suffering at the hands of men to flight into a trackless desert. There was a man who could have immunized himself against the treason of friends and the cowardice of enemies and who yet chose the least easy solution: he faced them directly. He opened his mind to them, exposed his sensibilities to them, and told them, "I am here and nowhere else!"

Yet Michael remained furious at the old man: idiot that you are, bloody fool! What are you trying to prove when you cling to others' values, others' judgments? That you're courageous? That you're human? That you aren't afraid of pain or injustice? That you insist on sanity? To whom are you justifying yourself? Of whom are you asking understanding or forgiveness? Why do you fear madness? Accept it, and rouse fear in others! Rouse fear in God himself! Accept madness, old man, take it, embrace it: that will be your protest against pain and injustice! Come, old man: Spit in their faces! Tell them, "If that's how you see life—thank you, but it's not for me!" Tell them, "If that's the sanity, the intelligence you're so proud of—not for me!" Go on, hopeless old man! Tell them what hurts! Are you afraid to leave them? Ashamed, perhaps?

But the old man lay prostrate and refused to listen.

* * *

Michael was awakened again one night by an attempted murder: the Impatient One had attacked the Silent One and was throttling him furiously. "Give me that letter! I know you've got it! That's why you don't talk! Give it to me!"

The boy was blue in the face, and his eyes were popping. He was not defending himself, and made no effort to struggle free. If Michael had awakened two minutes later he'd have found him dead. With surprising strength he leaped up and tried to separate them. But the Impatient One had the strength of a bloodthirsty animal. His fingers were clenched around the boy's neck like a pair of tongs: impossible to pry them open. With no time to waste, Michael grabbed his neck and squeezed; squeezed harder, still harder, and finally saw the killer release his prey.

Michael should have relaxed his own hold then, but for a fraction of a second he went on squeezing: his fingers refused to obey. He snapped out of it then and let the unconscious man fall.

That night Michael did not sleep. Pedro came to visit. He seemed more melancholy than usual. A bit more worried. He is dead or arrested, Michael thought.

"You saved a human life, little brother. I'm proud of you."

"I saved a body. A body with a sleeping mind and a dead soul. I'm not proud."

"Save his soul. You can do it."

"No, Pedro. I can't. I'm sinking fast too. A little while ago I almost killed a man. My own soul is blotting up madness and night. The whole universe has gone mad. Here and everywhere."

Pedro smiled: he was remembering something.

"You're smiling, Pedro, and I'm going mad. I have no strength left. I'm at the end of the line. I can't do any more. I'm alone. To stay sane I've got to have someone across from me. Otherwise my mind will rot, and smell of decay, and twist like the serpent that feels the earth and death."

Pedro went on smiling: "That's exactly what I want you to do: re-create the universe. Restore that boy's sanity. Cure him. He'll save you."

Pedro had come without his pipe. He was probably arrested or dead, and that was why he hadn't brought it. Ask him directly? I was afraid to. I didn't want to hear him say, "I've been arrested," or "I'm dead." I let him talk and didn't interrupt. He was saying, "The only valuable protest, or attitude, is one rooted in the uncertain soil of humanity. Remaining human—in spite of all temptations and humiliations—is the only way to hold your own against the Other, whatever it may be. Your Impatient One, waiting for a letter that no one will ever send him—what is he proving? Nothing at all. His behavior—however tragic—is as futile, as sterile, as a machine running in neutral. To see liberty only in madness is wrong: liberation, yes; liberty, no."

Michael welcomed the dawn as a new man. His strength flowed back. He was suddenly responsible for a life that was an inseparable part of the life of mankind. He would fight. He would resume the creation of the world from the void. *God of Adam and of Abraham, this time, I beg you, don't be against us!*

The Impatient One was transferred to another cell and Michael remained alone with his protégé. He changed corners immediately; now he was living where Menachem had lived.

During the first days he communicated only in gestures, and then by expressions; finally he used words too. The important thing was to establish an exchange, a rapport, of whatever kind.

In the morning—or the evening—he waited until the boy had drunk his coffee, and then offered his own. Absently the boy took the bowl and drained it. On the fourth or fifth day Michael, holding his breath, withheld the second bowl and waited: failure or success? It worked. The other, like a blind man, extended a hand and groped for something that belonged to him. The gesture moved Michael profoundly.

A few days later he pushed the experiment further: when the guard brought the two rations of coffee Michael took them both and hid them behind his back. The boy extended his right hand, then his left. Michael did not stir. He watched: would life suffuse that face, that stare? For a moment nothing happened. Absolute immobility. The earth ceased to turn, the blood to flow, the heart to beat.

And then the ice broke. A gleam—the first—split the opacity of those eyes. Michael glimpsed human thirst, human suffering, a human question: "Why are you torturing me?"

Tears in his eyes, Michael proffered the still-warm drink.

He repeated the trick with bread, with water, with soup. The boy's reflexes grew fuller and quicker. After a time his body responded: Yes, I'm thirsty; yes, I'm hungry; yes, I need you so that I can eat and drink. It was language on an animal level, physical, but Michael was full of hope: the rest would come. He had broken down one wall, that of the senses: the boy was aware of his presence. As a first result, that was not negligible. But the battle was far from finished; it would be full of difficulties and Michael had only himself to call upon.

At times he was on the verge of despondency: Will I one day pierce that wall, dispel those murky shadows? This boy has a past; will I ever know about it? His silence veils joys, fears, hopes, women's kisses, humiliations inflicted by "grownups"; will it shatter for me? Michael knew nothing save what those eyes could tell him: was he at least capable of speech, or understanding? Did he have a name? Had he ever had an identity? Relentlessly he persevered. The means at his disposition were poor: the cave man had

had better. Not even a scrap of iron or a sharp stone for drawing pictures on the walls. Michael did not lose heart. I have nothing? No matter. I can push back the night with my bare hands. I'll kill the black spider in prey of our silence.

As soon as he was sure that the boy was seeing him, he became a changed man.

To set the boy an example he danced, laughed, clapped hands, scratched himself with his dirty nails, made faces, stuck out his tongue: he had to show the boy that being a man meant all this.

Now he talked all day long, sang through endless evenings. He told sad stories and let his tears run freely: when a man is troubled, he weeps. He told erotic stories, even obscene stories, while his cheeks flamed like torches at twilight: desire is fire and strength. He reported funny adventures he had lived through or heard about, and laughed in great gusts: laughter is a weapon.

The boy listened silently, immobile as a statue, resisting all assaults. Words, tears, Michael's funny faces were flung up against him and fell back like dead birds.

Michael lost his temper often; then, his face wrathful, his eyes flashing sparks, he struck the boy violently or shook him by the shoulders until they were both out of breath.

"Wake up, for God's sake! It's our only chance! One of us will win and if it isn't me we're both lost! Do you hear me?"

Futile. The shaggy boy kept silence, breathing the air of another world.

Michael wept in impotent rage: "Help me, you bloody cretin! Make an effort! Snap out of it!"

Imperturbable, the other stared, as if all this were no concern of his.

Once Michael opened the boy's mouth by main

strength, pulling at his jaws with both hands: "Say something! Speak! One word, just one! Speak up!"

The other did not react. If he was in pain, he gave no sign. His eyes gazed through Michael as if they saw nothing.

"At least tell me your name!" Michael shouted, and gritted his teeth. "I am Michael. Are you listening? Michael! Pay attention, watch my lips: Mi-chael! And who are you? What's your name? Help me. It's silly, I know, but that's how it is. You're crazy, and I'm not, but only you can get us out of this. Give me some help, for God's sake! What's your name?"

Futile efforts, vain furies. The boy lived in a kingdom barred to Michael. Where he lived, tortures and caresses were of little effect. Michael therefore armed himself with fresh patience. He had to persevere at any cost.

The day when the boy suddenly began sketching arabesques in the air was one of the happiest of Michael's life. His eyes dimmed with tears. Then all was not inexorably lost and barren. He felt like dropping to his knees and offering thanks to God. He did not; but took the boy's hand in his own, squeezed it hard, very hard, and murmured gently, "Thank you, little one, thank you." His intelligence and personality were still dim, barely flickering, but Michael took heart.

Now he talked more, as if wishing to store ideas and values in the boy for his moment of awakening. Michael compared himself to a farmer: months separated the planting and the harvest. For the moment, he was planting.

"Right at this instant, little one, there are couples all over the world who think they're embracing, and some who really are; there are hearts hammering because they want to be beside someone who has just departed; and in the wild countryside of some country just awakening or just falling asleep there is a woman, some woman, being stoned for a reason, some reason, and nothing can save her from human beings; and there is a man, some man, being deserted, whatever his desires, and he can expect nothing more from human beings. And yet I tell you: affection exists; it is created and transmitted like a secret formula from heart to heart and from mouth to ear.

"I know: the paths of the soul, overgrown, often know only the night, a very vast, very barren night, without landscapes. And yet I tell you: we'll get out. The most glorious works of man are born of that night.

"I know, little one: it isn't easy to live always under a question mark. But who says that the essential question has an answer? The essence of man is to be a question, and the essence of the question is to be without answer.

"But to say, 'What is God? What is the world? What is my friend?' is to say that I have someone to talk to, someone to ask a direction of. The depth, the meaning, the very salt of man is his constant desire to ask the question ever deeper within himself, to feel ever more intimately the existence of an unknowable answer.

"Man has the right to risk life, his own life; he does not need to submerge himself in destiny in order to maintain his deep significance. He must risk, he can risk, a confrontation with destiny, he must try to seize what he demands, to ask the great questions and ask them again, to look up at another, a friend, and to look up again: if two questions stand face to face, that's at least something. It's at least a victory. The question, the demand, the outcry, the sickness in the soul or in the eyes—they never die.

"What I say to you, pass on to you, little one, I learned from a friend—the only one I had. He's dead, or in prison. He taught me the art and the necessity of clinging to humanity, never deserting humanity. The man who tries to be an angel only succeeds in making faces.

"It's in humanity itself that we find both our question and the strength to keep it within limits—or on the contrary to make it universal. To flee to a sort of Nirvana—whether through a considered indifference or through a sick apathy—is to oppose humanity in the most absurd, useless, and comfortable manner possible. A man is a man only when he is among men. It's harder to remain human than to try to leap beyond humanity. Accept that difficulty. Tell yourself that even God admits His weakness before the image he has created.

"To be indifferent—for whatever reason—is to deny not only the validity of existence, but also its beauty. Betray, and you are a man; torture your neighbor, you're still a man. Evil is human, weakness is human; indifference is not.

"They'll probably tell you that it's all only a play, that the actors are in disguise. So what? Jump onto the stage, mingle with the actors, and perform, you too. Don't stay at the window. Get out of the nest, but never try to reach the heights by flying away from thirsty children and mothers with milkless breasts. The real heights are like the real depths: you find them at your own level, in simple and honest conversation, in glances heavy with existence.

"One day the ice will break and you'll begin to smile: for me that will be a proof of our strength, of our compact. Then you'll shake yourself and the shadows will fall away from you as the fever leaves a sick man: you'll open your eyes and you'll say to yourself, 'I feel better, the sickness is gone, I'm different.' You'll tell me your name and you'll ask me, 'Who are you?' and I'll answer, 'I'm Pedro.' And that will be a proof that man survives, that he passes himself along. Later, in another prison, someone will ask your name and you'll say, 'I'm Michael.' And then you will know the taste of the most genuine of victories."

Michael had come to the end of his strength. Before him the night was receding, as on a mountain before dawn.

The other bore the Biblical name of Eliezer, which means *God has granted my prayer*.

LEGEND TELLS US THAT ONE DAY MAN SPOKE TO GOD IN
this wise:

"Let us change about. You be man, and I will be
God. For only one second."

God smiled gently and asked him, "Aren't you
afraid?"

"No. And you?"

"Yes, I am," God said.

Nevertheless he granted man's desire. He became a
man, and the man took his place and immediately
availed himself of his omnipotence: he refused to revert to his previous state. So neither God nor man was
ever again what he seemed to be.

Years passed, centuries, perhaps eternities. And suddenly the drama quickened. The past for one, and the
present for the other, were too heavy to be borne.

As the liberation of the one was bound to the liberation of the other, they renewed the ancient dialogue
whose echoes come to us in the night, charged with
hatred, with remorse, and most of all, with infinite
yearning.